LULA DARLING: A LIFE'S PURPOSE

ALEX DEAN

TREBOR & TAYLOR PUBLISHING

BOOKS BY ALEX DEAN

Lula Darling Series
Book 1: The Secret Life of Lula Darling
Book 2: A Life's Purpose

Alexis Fields Thrill Series
Restraining Order
The Bogeyman Next Door
Stalked

Alexis Fields - Complete Thrill Series Box Set

Standalone Books
The Client
A High-Stakes Crime Thriller

CHAPTER 1

I LAY RESTLESS in my bed, thinking about the past that Mama and I had left behind. The untimely deaths of my brother, Clarence, and my father, Luke. I still envisioned the terrors we'd endured and those who might have died in the now-infamous Mansfield Plantation fire.

There was so much I still had to learn about life in this century. There was also a great deal I wanted to forget about the past. A life at once filled with terror and tragedy in the deep antebellum South, and yet, through God's ultimate grace and mercy, we'd been delivered. Not only freed, but we were time travelers to a distant future.

For several minutes I stirred, before hearing what sounded like a series of groans emerging from the next room. I threw back the covers, then rose and rushed into the other bedroom to see about Mama.

Somehow she'd managed to end up on the floor beside her bed. I knelt beside her as she shivered, mumbling in fear, words that for the life of me I could not understand.

"Mama, please wake up!" I said as I gently shook her. With her head in a constant motion, stirring from side to side, suddenly, she opened her eyes.

"Mama, it's me, your baby girl, Lula," I said, putting a hand behind her back to lift her toward the bed. Mama took a deep breath as she sat up, grasping my arm for support. I noticed beads of sweat glistening around her forehead and wondered if she was in a panic.

"Better yet, let's go into the kitchen. I'll make you some tea. There we can talk, stay up and watch the sunrise. It's Saturday morning, and I don't have to work."

Mama nodded. She managed to get her feet beneath her and then trudged into the kitchen on weary legs. I poured some water in a kettle to boil and then we both sat at the kitchen table.

I believed that we were still haunted by the nightmares of slavery. I honestly suspected the appropriate condition today would be called post-traumatic stress disorder. And although most of the investigation by the CIA, NSA, and Department of Homeland Security was over, we still received an occasional phone call from an agent of some sort, asking us to recall something from the past.

The teakettle on the stove whistled. I reached into the cabinet for two mugs and then poured Mama and myself a cup of piping-hot organic green tea.

"I wish Daddy and Clarence could have seen what we got to see. The future. I wish they could have traveled through time with us," I said with heartfelt sadness.

Mama nodded as she lifted her cup. "Me too, baby girl."

I grabbed a glass jar of Manuka honey off the counter and sweetened my tea.

Mama took a sip of the hot beverage. "Can't do nothing but make the most of this blessing. I'm sure that's what your daddy would have wanted," she said.

I nodded slowly in agreement. Because on this

first official day of summer, while the outside world was still asleep, Mama and I were thinking about the life we wished we'd never known. But as I had been gloriously taught as a young girl whenever Mama quoted from the Bible, to everything there is a season and a time for every purpose.

As was to be expected, things were much better now. Mama was here, healthy and happier. I was now in college, with a new job and friends. And I still had my boyfriend, Marcus. We'd been dating since high school, and now, to absolutely no one's surprise, he'd become somewhat of a local celebrity.

I leaned back in my chair and smiled at the happy thoughts.

Suddenly, there was some discordant yelling outside, followed by the sound of fleeing footsteps. Mama and I exchanged a concerned look. I set my cup down on the table and hurried to the living room window.

Peeking out the curtains, I saw nothing but a typical gray Saturday morning in a neighborhood that had been slowly undergoing gentrification. A vacant lot littered with empty bottles, several broken-down cars, a stray homeless animal or two.

"It's not even well into the morning, and somebody's already acting up," I said, looking outside. "I can't wait to make enough money to move." I went back into the kitchen, cinched my bathrobe and sat down again.

Moments later the sound of gunfire echoed in the new silence.

"Mama, get down!" I yelled. We bolted off our seats and got down on our hands and knees, cowering on the floor. Then we crawled from the kitchen into the nearest bedroom. I circled around the bed to grab the phone from the nightstand to call the police.

Gang violence and drug dealing had been allowed to flourish on the South and West Sides. And I desperately wanted to be a part of the solution, not sit idly by watching black folks destroy themselves, this young generation. I wished that I could take them by the hand, back into time, during my early childhood in the antebellum South, so they could know firsthand how they had now become their own most familiar enemy.

I could hear the slam of a car door, then a woman screaming. Without hesitation, without another word, I rushed back to the front window and looked outside. There were at least four police cars, and an ambulance with its siren blaring, facing north toward downtown.

"I'm going outside, Mama!" I muttered as I slipped off my robe and pulled on a pair of jeans, a sweater, and sneakers.

Mama quickly grabbed my arm.

"Lula, I don't think you should be out there right now! We're still surrounded by danger. Got to watch out for what our own might do as much as we do for anyone else."

Looking in Mama's eyes, I saw a recurring pain across her face, newly formed creases brought about by worry and stress. "Now we came all this way, through hell and high water, for whatever God's purpose was for us to do. Don't be no fool by going out there and getting yourself killed tryin' to make it right!" Mama went on.

"I'll be okay, Mama. I feel it's what God put in my heart to do. I feel it's what *I* was put here to do. My life's purpose." I leaned over and gently kissed my mother on the cheek. Then I left my apartment and closed the door behind me.

Apparently several of my neighbors had heard the gunfire. Now that the police were outside, an older married couple, the Thomases, and I walked out of the building together toward the end of the block. As we approached, several local news vans pulled alongside a row of parked cars. There was a small crowd, which had gathered in front of the liquor store on the corner. The scene was crazy, like a gangland homicide off one of television's most popular cop shows. Looking between bystanders, on the ground, I saw a young man who looked no older than nineteen, lying in a coagulating pool of blood. Motionless. Lifeless.

A woman in a pink-and-gray jogging suit had to be restrained. It took one female and two male cops to keep her from breaching the crime scene. She wailed, her arms reaching forward in desperation, inconsolable. I assumed her to be the mother of the young man who'd been mercilessly gunned down.

Police ordered everyone away from the property as they covered his body. The first painful memory that had flooded my mind was that of Marcus lying on the ground when he had been shot not far from here.

Suddenly, after one of the policemen wrapped yellow tape around the scene, we were ordered to leave the premises. But before the crowd dispersed, a squat young twenty-something man pulled out his cell phone and began recording.

"Yeah, this right here is going on Facebook Live," he said.

"Give me that damn phone!" a nearby police sergeant growled. He wore a white shirt beneath what looked like a bulletproof vest. The man with the phone continued recording but started to move backward.

"This *my* phone! You can't tell me what to do with my phone!"

The cop bobbed under the tape, and the guy with the cell phone took off running. The officer reached for his holster and pulled out his gun, before another cop quickly and wisely stuck out his arm to lower the sergeant's aim. No one even bothered to give chase. This whole thing had seemed so surreal. The next thing I wondered was if the man lying on the ground had been shot and killed by the police, or by someone else in this neighborhood. Possibly a drug dealer or a gang rival.

I turned and looked at my neighbors as they stood several feet behind me. Mrs. Thomas shook her head in disgust as she and her husband headed back toward home. "That boy will just be another statistic in the city's ongoing war against crime," she said.

I nodded and acknowledged what my neighbor

had said. Her comment appeared to have come from a place of long-standing pain and discontent. "I couldn't agree with you more, Mrs. Thomas. Now the question is … what are we, as concerned people, going to do about it? We've marched, we've sung and protested peacefully. I say it's time we try something new."

CHAPTER 2

Early on a Sunday morning, the day before I would start my new job as a special education teacher's assistant, Mama D. graciously invited Mama and me to attend Pastor Tomkins's church in the historic neighborhood of Bronzeville.

Mama D. had also ordered Marcus to attend. I'd often heard her encourage him: "It's never too early, nor too late, for that matter, to form a long-lasting relationship with the Lord."

This was the first time that either Mama or myself had ever attended organized religious services of any kind. To us, this was a great privilege, being able to worship God as free women, without any fear of being punished for doing so.

After slipping into my clothes, I went to see if Mama needed any help putting on the floral dress that I'd purchased for her with what little money I had left after paying bills. I walked into the bathroom and saw her smile as she stood by the sink and studied herself in the mirror.

"You're lookin' really nice in that outfit. So young and pretty, people are gonna think we're sisters," I said and smiled.

"You think so?" Mama replied and whirled gracefully, then she smoothed out the wrinkles in her dress.

"Yes, I do. And who knows, Mama? You might even meet you a fine gentleman at that church."

My mother turned to me with a look of concern. "I'm a little nervous. Not sure what to expect. They tell you what goes on at these services?"

I gently grabbed Mama by her hand. "All I can say is ... it must be something special. Mama D. attends each and every Sunday. By some divine miracle, she even got Marcus to come with us this morning. Now let's go wait outside. They're supposed to be here any minute now."

Mama and I grabbed our purses, left our apartment and headed down two flights of creaking stairs. Once outside, we walked along the sidewalk and waited by the curb. Wide-eyed and curious, we looked like two gracious churchwomen that could've been serving plates at the Last Supper.

Minutes later and through an early-morning drizzle, Marcus and Mama D. pulled in front of my building on South Dr. Martin Luther King Jr. Drive. Marcus put his car in park, got out and then opened the back door. I assisted Mama into the backseat and then climbed in and sat beside her.

"You all are in for a real treat," Mama D. said enthusiastically as she munched contentedly on a bag of caramel corn. "Every first Sunday of the month, there is a visiting choir, food, and each and every week we make it a priority to make our visitors feel really welcome."

Mama D. then swiveled her head toward the backseat and said, "I take it you all have never been to a real church?"

"No, ma'am," Mama and I said in unison.

"Well, I've been a member of the First Deliverance Baptist Church of Bronzeville for nearly seventeen years. Pastor Tompkins usually has a church bus come and pick me up since I don't drive. But this morning I was able to talk my grandson into going and taking us there. I've always told him he was never too young to know the Lord."

"Can't nobody say I ain't never been to

church!" Marcus said boldly. He shook his head and smiled. Then he glanced at Mama D., and almost paraded right through a red light. He quickly caught himself, put the car in reverse and backed up.

"Watch where you're going, boy! We'd all like to get there in one piece," Mama D. spat out with a hearty laugh.

Once the light turned green, Marcus accelerated, negotiated a sharp right, then traveled down the block and pulled into the church's side parking lot. As soon as the car's front tires hit the asphalt, a clean-cut young man wearing black slacks and a gray shirt opened the car's back door and then directed us toward the front of the building.

Mama D. struggled to get out. "Wait! Everybody, slow down. This old bird can't quite move as fast as she used to. Marcus, grab my arm," Mama D. blurted, and Marcus assisted her out of the car. With cane in hand and Marcus flanking her side, she got to her feet and shuffled beside Mama and me toward the church's entrance.

Before going inside, Mama and I stood still for a moment, taking in the large blue-and-white sign that hung proudly over the doorway: 1ST DELIVERANCE   BAPTIST   CHURCH   OF

BRONZEVILLE, Reverend E.L. Tompkins, Senior Pastor.

Pastor Tompkins was widely known and admired in this neighborhood for doing what he could to help the less fortunate. But Marcus had his doubts. One day, while we were holed up in his recording studio, Marcus had told me that Reverend Tompkins had had a shady past. Allegedly, Reverend Tompkins had taken some kind of bribe while working on a city job he'd held before becoming pastor of the church. Although the money was said to be in the tens of thousands, somehow he had managed to avoid any jail time.

The castle-like wooden door was opened for the four of us, and Mama and I walked in behind Marcus and Mama D. The smell of food cooking somewhere in the building pleasantly met us as soon as we stepped in. Black folks called it soul food. White folks called it comfort food. But to me, it was all the same. Delicious, even though eating it, we'd been warned, could often cause you problems.

Mama and I noted everything. The women who were seated in various pastel colors. The wooden beams that crossed along the ceiling. The windows that ringed the top of the room. The elevated platform, podium, and microphone that took up the front of the sanctuary. There was even a set of shiny and colorful instruments off to the right.

"This is amazing," Mama muttered.

A sweet-looking older woman, probably in her eighties, escorted us down the aisle near the front of the church. She held out her hand, directing us where to sit.

Mama D. stood to the side, allowing us to be seated first. "Since you all are my guests, I put in a special request with Reverend Tompkins to allow us to sit near the front. Looks like he accommodated us," she said exuberantly. The four of us sat down, with Mama D. at row's end near the aisle for an easy exit, in case she 'needed to make a quick trip to the ladies room,' as she had told us.

I turned to my right and saw Mama being greeted and welcomed by another parishioner. Mama smiled and leaned over and said, "Still can't believe how we've come so far so fast."

I had to remind her that it wasn't fast. Though you could argue that it *was* quite liberating, especially coming from the annals of history in 1852.

Over the past twelve months, I'd taught Mama everything I could about this present-day life. How to speak appropriately. How to dress and use modern-day technology. The major differences between twentieth- and twenty-first century life.

But still, there was more we had to learn.

The congregation quieted down as Reverend Tompkins walked up to the podium. Three young men followed him and took their places behind the instruments that sat on the stage. Drums, keyboards, and guitars. I had learned more about making music than I ever cared to by spending so much time in Marcus's studio.

The musicians began playing softly, and the music was nothing but soothing to my ears.

I briefly closed my eyes and meditated on the sound.

"Let us give God some praise this Sunday morning! Isn't He worthy?" Reverend Tompkins blurted over the music, as it suddenly grew louder.

"Yes! Yes!"

I looked on the left side of the room and behind me. There were people standing, shouting, raising their hands toward the sky. Suddenly Mama rose and did the same. Marcus, Mama D., and I quickly stood on our feet as well. I looked over at Mama's face and saw her eyes well up. This was the most emotional that I had seen her since the day we'd been reunited.

Over the next hour, Reverend Tompkins spoke eloquently and passionately on God's grace and mercy and the importance of us finding His purpose for our lives. After his moving sermon and the swell of gospel music, the reverend invited anyone who might want to come on the stage to come up and offer a testimony.

I was shocked when Mama looked at me and said that she was going to go up and do just that.

She stood, and the same sweet lady who had helped us to our seats escorted Mama up to the platform. Reverend Tompkins, in his dark blue double-breasted suit, leaned over and hugged Mama intensely. Then he stepped aside and sat down behind her. Mama looked out at the sea of faces in the congregation.

"I want to thank Reverend Tompkins and the Whitaker family for inviting me and my wonderful daughter, Lula, to join you all this Sunday morning. My daughter and I have a very unique testimony that could only be attributed to God's mercy and His majestical power." Mama cleared her throat and then continued. "As hard as it may be for everyone here to believe, my daughter and I were born in the 1800s as slaves and traveled here to experience this life."

Most of the church erupted in laughter. I looked around the entire sanctuary, at as many faces as I could, completely dismayed. Marcus simply glanced at me and shrugged. I couldn't believe that Mama was about to tell others, complete strangers, our most closely guarded secret. But just as soon as she started to spill the beans, she smiled and quickly reversed her course of action.

Mama chuckled and then paused for a moment. "Now that I've got you all's attention, I just want to say that God has truly brought my daughter and me through some hard times, even reunited us when we lost contact with each other. But as I taught her when she was a little girl, always put God first in your life, and never, not ever, give up faith in what only He can do. Thank you."

There was a surge of applause and intense clapping, several shouts of complete joy and total happiness as Mama stepped away from the pulpit. Reverend Tompkins stood up and echoed the sentiment. He beamed proudly, clapped, adjusted his glasses and gave Mama another great big inviting hug.

At the conclusion of the worship service, Marcus and Mama D. took us home, where I served up a nice Sunday dinner. It had already been decided that instead of joining the church's members for supper in the fellowship room, we would simply have our own. For the rest of the evening, all Mama and I could talk about was how nice 1st Deliverance had been, how great Reverend Tompkins's sermon was, how everyone had embraced us, making us feel so special. We could not wait to attend again.

We had finally found our church home.

CHAPTER 3

MARCUS and I returned from picking up groceries and carried six bags into the kitchen, where Mama D. had been waiting on us to cook dinner. For several days, there had barely been any food in the house, and Mama D. wanted to serve up a good home-cooked meal that the three of us could sit down and really sink our teeth into.

After touring the Midwest with his rap group and entourage, Marcus had returned home last night for a break in between cities. He'd always felt torn between pursuing his dream and being here for the only two people who had ever seemed to care about him. All at once, he seemed amped up and giddy, if that were even possible.

Mama D. was glad to have him here, too. The only two people that she could depend on running errands during the day had been Marcus and, on occasion, Pastor Tompkins. But the real reason why she missed him so much was because she truly loved her grandson.

I followed Marcus into the kitchen, where we put food in the refrigerator and canned goods in the pantry. When I returned to the living room, Mama D. was lying on the sofa with one leg elevated, perched on top of a chair. Her eyes were closed. She did not look well and seemed short of breath.

"Mama D.? What's wrong? Anything I can do for you?" I asked as I drew closer to the couch.

Mama D. winced in pain. "I just need to rest, that's all. But thank you for asking, Lula. My leg has suddenly decided that it don't wanna cooperate. I'm a diabetic."

Concerned, I immediately walked out of the living room and into the kitchen. Marcus had been busy rearranging food to put more into the freezer. "Mama D.'s not well. I think you need to come and see about her," I said.

Marcus quickly slammed the door to the freezer and followed me into the living room, where Mama D. was holding her leg now. He knelt by the sofa and grabbed his grandmother's hand. "You're not well, Mama D. I'm calling for an ambulance."

"No. Boy, I don't need to go to no hospital! They ain't gonna do nothing but keep me for a few days and tell me what I already know!"

Marcus wasn't having it. He went across the room and grabbed the telephone to dial 911. "I'm calling them anyway. You haven't been eating right, and you need to go to the emergency room."

Against Mama D.'s wishes, Marcus summoned paramedics, and they arrived roughly eight minutes later. A man and a woman got out of the ambulance, grabbed a medic kit, then rolled out a steel gurney and started toward the house. They carried the gurney up the front porch and into the living room. After asking Mama D. a few questions, they moved her on top of the stretcher, strapped her down, and then took her down the steps.

"You can follow us in my car, Lula." Marcus tossed me his keys before he left out and climbed in the back of the ambulance. I closed and then locked the front door of the house before I got in Marcus's SUV to trail them to the emergency room.

Moments later, we arrived at Chicago Advocate Hospital. The closer I got to actually going inside, the more nervous I became, fearing the worst. But first I had to find a place to park. I pulled into the first visitor's parking lot I saw, parked, and then rushed into the emergency room waiting area.

Marcus saw me as soon as I rushed in. "Fortunately, they've already got Mama D. being looked at by a doctor. I'm waiting until they say we can go in," he said over nervous breath. The first time I'd ever seen the inside of a hospital was the day Marcus had been shot outside of a frat house during a party for graduating seniors. And now here I was again, hoping and praying for his grandmother, a big-hearted woman who, without question, held a special place in my heart. I slipped Marcus's hand in mine and stood beside him as we waited for some kind of positive word.

I scanned the ER as patients were being wheeled in. Nurses and several doctors walked by us in opposite directions. Concerned family members checked at the nurses' station for up-to-the-minute information.

"Man, I hope she's gonna be all right," Marcus said, crestfallen as he shifted his gaze toward the floor.

"Yeah, I hope so too. I know how much she means to you," I said.

"She's all I got, Lula. Well, besides you, of course." Marcus blew out a breath and rested his head back against the wall. "I feel kind of bad that I've been gone as long as I have. It's only been several weeks, but I know she ain't been eating right. I *know* she hasn't," he said, shaking his head.

Marcus stood off the wall. "It's been almost an hour, and I haven't heard anything. I'm going to check and see just what is going on."

"I'll go with you." I followed Marcus to a desk where a nurse in blue scrubs was sitting, looking at a screen.

"How are you, ma'am? My name is Marcus, and I wanted to see if we could check on my grandmother to see how she's doing. Her name is Delores Whitaker."

"Give me a moment. Let me check with Maribel, she's the nurse on duty."

The woman stood, walked away from the desk and went down the hall. I saw her talking to several other nurses as she nodded her head. I took that as a sign that perhaps we would finally get to see Mama D. When she returned to her desk, she pointed in the direction from which she had returned.

"The doctor has ordered some tests, and we're awaiting the results." The nurse smiled. "But right now your grandmother's resting comfortably. You can go in. She's in room 110E."

Marcus and I made a beeline for the room.

When we entered, Mama D. brightened, smiling when she saw us. Marcus and I leaned over, gave her a heartfelt hug, then stood by her bed. Various types of medical devices surrounded her, including a blood pressure monitor, which beeped every few seconds.

Marcus and I pulled two chairs forward from the corner of the room and sat next to the bed. "Now, aren't you glad you came here?" he asked matter-of-factly.

Mama D. shook her head in protest. "Nope. The food ain't nothin' like what I can cook at home or get out in the street."

"Yeah, that's the problem. I know you ain't been eating right! You probably had Mr. Foster running to get you some fried chicken, French fries, and diet soda all the time while I was gone."

"Who's Mr. Foster?" I asked.

Marcus shot me a glance. "He's our next-door neighbor."

Mama D. smiled. "Well, I'm allowed to treat myself every now and then, aren't I? Look how you eat. You hardly ever eat at home."

Marcus shook his head and smiled as he straightened Mama D.'s blanket. "What am I going to do with you? I'm not trying to see you leave up outta here anytime soon. Now stop being hard-headed, will you?"

I admired the playful relationship Marcus had with his grandmother, and it was obvious how much they loved one another.

"Lula, can you turn that TV channel up?" Mama D. asked, pointing toward the edge of the bed. "I don't wanna miss a rerun of Steve Harvey and *Family Feud*."

"Sure." I grabbed the remote-looking device, which was out of Mama D.'s reach. As soon as I turned up the volume, a man walked into the room. I lowered the volume back down.

"Hello, I'm Dr. Sabharwald," he said, extending his hand to shake Marcus's and then mine. "Ms. Whitaker, you are a very popular person. You've got people who care about you!" he announced with a foreign accent.

"Yes, I'm blessed that I have a grandson who cares about me. His name is Marcus, and that's his girlfriend there, Lula."

I smiled and gave a friendly wave.

"Well, your test results are back, and we need to

work on getting some better numbers. Your blood sugar level is currently over five hundred. You're very fortunate you did not have a stroke. Have you been eating correctly and taking care of yourself?"

Mama D. shook her head. "Not always, Doctor."

"Well, maybe this is your wake-up call to take better care of yourself. We're going to keep you for three or four days and try to get your numbers down."

Marcus looked at his grandmother. "You hear that, Mama D.? You've got to start eating better. All the time!"

The doctor looked at Marcus and I. "That's the problem concerning diabetes. A lot of people don't respect the disease and therefore do not eat accordingly." The doctor then turned back to Mama D. "You're going to have to eat to live instead of living to eat, Ms. Whitaker. You don't want to go through having a limb amputated, blindness or worse. Do you have a glucose meter?"

"Yes, I have one, just have to remember to use it every night after I eat my dinner."

"You'll definitely want to do that. My guess is you were probably close to having a stroke had your grandson not urged you to get to the emergency room. You're lucky to have him there keeping an eye on you."

"Well, I appreciate having him around. Not sure what I'd do without him or his wonderful girlfriend here, Lula."

"I'll let you rest and enjoy your grandson and his girlfriend. I'll be back to check on you periodically, okay?"

Mama D. nodded. "All right, Doctor."

Marcus and I stayed with Mama D. until visiting hours were over. By that time, she had fallen asleep and did not even budge when nurses came into the room. We planned to return here in the morning and were hoping that Mama D. would be given new, more acceptable test results. Either way, come hell or high water, we were going to be present. Being around Ariel when her grandmother was sick, I had seen firsthand how crucial it was for staff to know and see that a patient's family actually cared.

Marcus leaned over and affectionately kissed Mama D. on her cheek. He pulled up the blanket to cover her upper body, and then we said goodnight.

CHAPTER 4

Marcus and I headed back to his house after leaving Mama D.'s bedside. When we arrived, the house was dark, and the curtains were still open. I followed Marcus inside and, upon entering, was bummed out by the lack of Mama D.'s usual warm and inviting presence.

I switched on the living room's ceiling light and then the TV. Marcus heated up some leftovers, and we took our plates back into the front room and sat on the couch.

"I'm just glad we made it back when we did," he said, sounding relieved.

"Why?" I asked.

"Cause you ain't gonna leave a house empty in pitch-black darkness around here and expect your stuff to still be here when you get back. Plus, we don't have an alarm system."

"Well, you need to get one, or better yet, once you start making big money, you can buy Mama D. a nice house in a nice neighborhood. Maybe out in the suburbs."

"Yeah, that's exactly what they want us to do. Haven't you ever heard of gentrification?"

"Yes. Of course, I've heard of gentrification. It's taking place all over the country. Even where I live. I see the area slowly changing, one house at a time. It's a shame everything has to be about money."

"Speaking of money, whatever happened to all the money you and your mother were supposed to receive for telling your stories?"

"Unfortunately, as part of our arrangement with the powers that be in Washington, we had to sign nondisclosure agreements. Can you imagine us sitting there, my mother not knowing how to read or write? I had to guide her hand just to get her name on the dotted line. We had to agree not to tell anyone else about our past. And believe it or not, they're still in contact with us periodically. We have to go back to Fort Meade for ongoing testing, blood work, you name it. All for before-and-after comparisons regarding our arrival here from the past. They want to know how the environment and time itself could have affected the molecular structure of our blood and DNA."

Marcus glared at me and cocked his head to one side. "Are you serious? I thought all that investigation stuff was behind you," he said. "Man, this is like the hood's version of *The X-Files*."

"It's not funny, Marcus."

"Who said it was funny?"

"You didn't say it, but you act like it's a joke! You have no idea what testing my mother and I had to go through."

Marcus shook his head. "No. I don't. Care to enlighten me?"

I stood up and looked out the window. For all I knew, the CIA, NSA or Department of Homeland Security could have me under surveillance, especially with the seeds of social activism that had now sprouted within my conscious. I needed to feel like he had my back. But it was times like this that, to me, Marcus showed a glaring lack of maturity. I sat back down next to him and looked him squarely in the face.

"This is completely off the record, between you and me only. My mother and I were subjected to a battery of psychological tests. We were also examined from the top of our heads to the soles of our feet, including having blood samples drawn, along with having cells from our skin and strands of our hair taken for an in-depth lab analysis. Then they took X-rays of our bodies, examining all of our major organs. We were there for an entire week. There is no telling what was put in our food or water. And on top of all that, we still have to submit ourselves to periodic testing for at least a two-year period from the date of the first test."

"What for?"

"I told you earlier. In simpler terms, they want to see what changes have occurred to our bodies in today's environment compared to that in which we lived in 1852. But me personally? I don't need any high-tech equipment to see and smell the difference. The first thing I remember upon my arrival was the smell of this rotted air. You know how... when you cut open an apple, and it slowly starts to turn brown? Well, from what I recall, that process didn't occur as fast in the nineteenth century. This air, with the pollution we breathe, is something alto-gether different. I hate to say it, but I think I've gotten used to it now."

Marcus gently grabbed my hand, leaned over and kissed my cheek. "I'm sorry. Didn't mean to offend you. I had no idea you and your mother had to endure all that. How is your mother doing now?"

"She's okay. Still has moments where she thinks of my father and little brother. She wishes they could've experienced this miracle with us. Slowly, she's been learning how to adapt to the present. It's funny—at first she would always cower in white folks' presence, but after seeing a black woman curse out a white manager in the grocery store the other day, I think Mama has had her aha moment."

Marcus picked up the remote and started to flip through channels. "You want to know what I think about all this? You want to hear my honest opinion?" he said.

I nodded. "Yes, please."

"Well, I think people need to know about you and your mother's past and how God brought you here. I think you should stop withholding what could be an inspiration to others. Especially the younger generation. Are you kidding me? These people out here have lost their damn minds!"

"I can't do that!"

"Why? You scared?"

"I don't want anything to happen to either me or Mama. And I definitely don't want to go to jail."

Marcus suddenly went into overdrive. "Lula,

you can find a way to do it subtly. Although, if you really care about social activism and doing something good for the betterment of people, you have to be willing to take a stand for what you actually believe in, just like the great leaders who came before you, even if that means someone else has to be uncomfortable."

I stared at Marcus and had to seriously consider what he had just said to me. On the Mansfield Plantation, under the extreme control and constant threat of brutality, neither Mama nor I had ever worried much about slave patrollers whenever they were rumored to be in the area or had spontaneously searched our cabins. With our faith, we had been confident in our ability to rise above all fears then. And I believed that that same seed of courageousness still lay within me now, a whole century later. Everyone else saw this world changing in slow, evolving paces. I saw the world changing much more rapidly, like a train speeding toward the side of a mountain with reckless abandon. We as a people, for the most part, had gotten alarmingly off track.

Marcus and I leaned our heads back against the sofa and watched *Jimmy Kimmel Live!* before nodding off into la-la land. At twelve a.m. sharp, my cell phone's alarm woke us. Slowly, I opened my eyes, my pupils adjusting to the light from the television bathing the living room. I eased myself forward on the couch, glanced at my cell phone's screen, and quickly asked Marcus to take me home. I imagined that Mama had been up waiting. I worried about her being alone in my apartment as much as I'm sure she worried about me being out in these streets.

CHAPTER 5

I'D DESPERATELY NEEDED a car to get back and forth to work and school. Marcus had told me about an older model that one of his neighbors urgently wanted to sell, a gray 2010 Nissan Sentra. After graduating last year and saving close to three thousand dollars from a summer job with the Chicago Park District, I'd bought it with a hope and a prayer that I could at least get a good two years out of it.

Adding to my stress was the fact that now Mama was ready to drive.

She'd been bored with staying in my apartment while I was gone and was tired of having to travel on public transportation. So I'd promised her that on this morning, I would be the first person ever to teach her how to drive. Mama was eager to learn the basics of operating a vehicle so that she could get her driver's license. I also tried in vain to get Ariel and Marcus to join in on this morning's expedition, but neither would commit. I wondered if they were scared of what could happen with Mama behind the wheel.

I left my bedroom, keys in hand, and grabbed a Granny Smith apple from the fridge.

"Mama, are you ready?"

"Yes. Be right there."

Several minutes later Mama appeared in a denim jacket over a white summer dress, wearing a pair of low-top sneakers that I had purchased on what we could only guess might have been her birthday. Mama knew when I was born, but we had no official way of knowing when she had entered the world, so we had simply chosen a month, day, and year out of thin air. That suited us.

"There's a big parking lot at an abandoned strip mall on the far South Side. I figured it'll be enough space for you to practice going forward, backing up, making turns, and, well, making mistakes without hopefully killing anybody," I told her.

Mama looked down and fastened the snaps on her jacket. "I'm not killin' nobody," she said. "But if I *were* going to get someone—I'd go back in time with some of these modern-day gizmos and go see that overseer."

I had a good long laugh at that one.

Leaving my second-floor apartment, we started down creaking and stained carpeted stairs. We walked out of the building and down a concrete porch to the curb, where my car, with its rapidly dulling paint and barely working air conditioner, awaited us.

I was still nervous about getting onto the Dan Ryan Expressway, which would have gotten us there a lot faster. So instead, we headed west over to Halsted, the longest-running street in the city, then made a left turn and started south to 115th Street.

The parking lot was a huge deserted block-wide space where a small indoor mall and an adjacent grocery store had done business in the community of Maple Park many years ago. Marcus had told me about this location when I'd first mentioned that I wanted to teach Mama how to drive.

He'd told me that, before opening his studio, he'd come out here three days a week to rehearse in the moldy basement of a friend, who also happened to be a musician turned rapper. As we pulled into the lot and onto the crumbling pavement, the first thing we noticed was the unmistakable presence of another group of people.

There was a row of several tables covered with white cloth in the middle of the lot. Each table had a handwritten sign attached to its front, which read: STOP THE VIOLENCE! Manning the tables were two men, three women, and several teenagers, all holding clipboards and wearing yellow T-shirts.

One of the men was speaking loudly through a bullhorn. We sat motionless for several minutes and watched. Moments later a small crowd had gathered.

"Looks like we got company, Mama. But we can do our business on the side. We won't get in their way," I said, surveying the scene.

Mama nodded, leaned over and gazed out the window. "We better hurry. Soon we may run out of room," she said.

I quickly opened the driver's-side door. Mama got out of her side, and we traded places. Her in the driver's seat, me as her passenger. We buckled our seat belts, then I went into instruction mode.

"Now this is the gear shift. P is for park. N is for neutral. R is for reverse and D is for drive," I said, pointing to the gear handle between our seats. Then I pointed toward the floor to show Mama which pedal was for the gas and which was for the brake. She glanced down with both feet planted firmly on the floor as I continued to explain.

"Now put your foot on the brake, press down, then take the gear handle and slowly shift it into drive." Mama did as I instructed. "Now gently take your foot off the brake and put it on the gas pedal."

The car jerked and slowly we moved forward. Mama kept two hands on the steering wheel and smiled. For roughly forty-five minutes we practiced going forward and backward. Turning and stopping. Eventually, we slowed and then stopped, with the car now facing the abandoned mall. Mama switched gears and kept her foot on the brake, waiting for my next instruction to back up as the car idled. She turned and looked at me, beaming like a child just given a handful of candy.

"I think I got the hang of it, baby girl! With a lil' more practice, I think I'll be ready to get my license. Start driving. Maybe even get me a car one day."

I turned, smiled and nodded. "That would be—"

"Ahhh!" Mama suddenly screamed. A teenager had violently slapped his hands on the driver's-side window, then frantically yelled, "*Hey!*"

Mama, in a panic, slammed on the gas pedal, and we went sailing backward toward the growing group of gathered people. As we neared them, the crowd desperately parted—not unlike the story of Moses and God's miracle at the Red Sea. People were scattering everywhere as my car crashed into tables, folding chairs, knocking clipboards and bottled water into the air.

Mama, finally realizing what she had done, stomped on the brake, bringing the car to a complete stop. Then she put the car in park. A tall man with a mustache and goatee, walking with a limp and a cane, was the first of several people to approach our car as me and Mama got out.

"What in God's name is your problem? You almost killed us with your no-driving self! Here we are, out here protesting against violence in the community, and almost get ran the hell right over!"

"I'm *so* sorry, sir. I was out here teaching my mother how to drive, when one of these young men scared the dickens out of her, causing her to slam her foot on the gas pedal."

Seeing the anger in their faces, Mama took several steps forward. She put her hand over her heart. "Please forgive me. In all my years of being on this earth, it's my very first time *ever* being behind the wheel of a car. I'm truly sorry," she said, scanning the crowd. "I hope everyone is all right."

An overweight woman wearing a red, yellow, and orange tube top with matching red shorts walked in front of the crowd, wagging a finger at us. "Fortunately, everybody is okay. But you need to practice somewhere where there's no people around," she scolded.

"Let us help you," Mama said, and the two of us helped set their tables upright, shook the table-cloths free of dust, and picked up most of the folding chairs that lay on the ground.

"What does your organization do?" I asked the man with the cane as most of the people who'd been working the table took their seats.

"We're a group of community activists trying to raise awareness regarding the violence that plagues our community. No one else seems to be stepping up. So we're planning on having a series of town hall meetings around the city."

"Where are the meetings? And when?" I asked.

"At various locations, churches, schools, community centers—basically, whoever will have us."

"I have an interest in doing the same. How can I help?" I said.

"Where do you live?"

"In Bronzeville," I replied.

"Well, we don't have much of an ongoing presence in Bronzeville. You know of a place where we can get folks to come out?"

At this very moment, a lightbulb went off in my head. The first place I thought of was Reverend Tompkins's church. *Perhaps Mama D. could ask him, seeing that it's a worthy cause*, I thought.

"I think I might have a place in mind," I said.

He reached down into a cooler and pulled out two ice-cold bottles of water. "Here's some water for you and your mother. My name's George Frazier, but everybody calls me Boogie," he said, extending his hand.

I chuckled. "Boogie? How'd you get that name?"

"I go out dancing a lot, mostly steppin'. Been doing it ever since I can remember. It's a way to take a break from the stress and monotony of life. All my neighbors and the people who grew up on my block remember that most about me, the dancing. I'm pretty good too!" Boogie suddenly stood up, leaning to one side on his cane. "Here's my card. I'm also on Facebook. Look forward to hearing from you. We need more socially conscious young people like yourself stepping up," he said.

I nodded. "Yeah, I agree. We've got to stop the bloodshed. I'll definitely be in touch."

More people had started to come off 115th Street to stop by and ask questions. Mama and I said our goodbyes and then got in the car. I cautiously pulled out of the parking lot and made a left turn, and then we headed north on Halsted. But no sooner than we had moved through the intersection, the air conditioner stopped working. We lowered the windows to compensate as a gentle breeze caressed our faces. There was nothing playing on the radio now except for commercials. But after the unexpected turn of events we'd experienced this morning, Mama and I yearned to hear some traveling music to put our minds at ease. So Mama snapped on her seat belt and began crooning the first bar of one of her favorite Negro spirituals: "Swing Low, Sweet Chariot," one of the most popular songs in slaves' quest for freedom during the Underground Railroad. I joined in and sang along.

Our life definitely wasn't perfect, or where I'd hoped it would be in the not-too-distant future. But it certainly wasn't too shabby for two former slaves finding our way in the twenty-first century.

CHAPTER 6

AFTER A HOPE and a prayer and a series of phone calls, Mama D. had made it happen. She had arranged with Pastor Tompkins to allow a town hall meeting at his church for the residents of Bronzeville, and any other concerned citizens on the South Side who wanted to attend.

Pastor Tompkins had also notified the local media, and I was surprised to see that at least three local stations had actually sent a news crew over for taping. Attending tonight were Mama D., Marcus, Ariel and her parents, and of course, Boogie, and the rest of his organization from the area he called The Wild 100's.

At almost a quarter to seven, residents slowly filed in and one of Pastor Tompkins's assistants instructed several cameramen to stand near the back of the sanctuary and move along the center aisle as needed. Also in attendance, I noted, were several officers of the Chicago Police Department, as well as pastors from other churches and several staff from the mayor's office.

This was an open-floor forum. Aldermen and department heads would be taking questions from the community while trying to determine if solutions could be raised to quell the city's epidemic of gun violence. Twenty minutes into the session, I was surprised to see the mayor himself come into the building, flanked by his security detail.

After several panelists spoke and took questions from the audience, the mayor made his way through a group of supporters and ventured onto the stage.

That was when things took a crazy and tumultuous turn.

A tall, intimidating silver-haired man with a pockmarked face, who described himself as a Vietnam veteran, listened intently as the mayor outlined his plan for jobs and economic development, then shouted, "Where is the help you've promised us for years?" He pointed at the stage.

"We've gotten nothing from you or your office but lip service, Mr. Mayor. All you're capable of doing is political posturizing!"

The mayor offered a thin smile but was clearly rattled. He scooped up several sheets of paper from the top of the podium. "Sir, I'd be happy to show you the numbers. You want to see them? We've had more companies investing in our city in the last two years than the previous eight combined," he went on. "Overall, crime is down in certain districts. There's been a decrease in unemployment. And—"

"Not in our neighborhood!" an older woman in a wheelchair yelled from the third row of pews. "I know what neighborhoods you're talking about. What about us?"

Another man, fifty-something and wearing some kind of dark blue delivery uniform, stood. "These kids, they need jobs out here, Mr. Mayor. 'Cause the ones that wanna be something are falling victim to the thugs and the gangbangers you keep letting out of jail. That group right there? They ain't never gonna amount to nothing!"

The mayor raised his hands in the air as if to calm the crowd.

"Okay. Each and every one of you, I hear your

concerns. I can assure you that the City of Chicago is investing in infrastructure and economic development and making changes within the police department, implementing strategies to reduce crime, starting in the most dangerous neighborhoods, where murders and violent crimes are the highest."

The wheelchair-bound woman raised her fist in the air and yelled over pleas for the crowd to settle down. "Well, you're also closing down our schools. Kids are dropping out, failing, with no hope for the future!"

The mayor looked to the side of the church as he shook his head in disagreement. Then he signaled for one of his aides to come to the pulpit as he whispered in her ear. The next thing I knew, I was being asked to go to the front of the sanctuary. Apparently, someone in the mayor's entourage had recognized me from my speech at Soldier Field and told the mayor that I was here.

"Lula? Where's Lula Darling?" he said, scanning the room. At the urging of several staffers, I made my way through the crowd, past several cameramen, and approached the pulpit. Once onstage, I stood beside the mayor as he put his hand on my shoulder.

"We have closed some underperforming

schools. But for the students who want an education and a promising future, the door of opportunity is wide open. This lovely young lady here is a testament to what can be accomplished with a desire to learn. She was valedictorian last year and gave the commencement speech at Soldier Field. Lula, would you like to say a few words?" the mayor asked me.

I nodded, feeling my heartbeat escalate. The mayor coyly left the pulpit and went across the room to talk to some reporters he had recognized. I looked over the crowd of riled faces and had to swallow hard. This would be the first time that I'd spoken in front of an audience of any size since my high school graduation. Although this crowd was much smaller, the atmosphere was more intense than I could have ever imagined. I struggled to find the appropriate words for the moment.

"I just want to say that I'm an example of what a CPS student can achieve given a chance to attend a great school with awesome teachers. As the mayor said, I graduated last year as valedictorian and am now attending DePaul University while also working as a special education assistant."

A middle-aged woman stood up from one of the

pews and walked out to the center of the aisle. "What high school did you attend, young lady?"

"Chicago Prep Academy," I replied.

The lady looked around the room shaking her head. "That's a good school. A new school. And no disrespect to you or your accomplishments, but most kids on the South and West Sides have a much harder road to travel."

Her comment made me angry. If I said nothing else the entire evening, I had to respond to this woman's condescending statement. "You don't know me. You don't know what obstacles I had to overcome," I told her.

Her face grew into an expression of animation. "I know enough about the demographics of this city to know where you had to live in order to attend *that* school. What are you, anyway, eighteen? Nineteen? Try learning about the real struggles of our people throughout history, continuing on till today. Consider yourself fortunate," the woman spat before taking her seat.

Her words hit me with the force of a blow. I felt my eyes fill with tears. "I know about the struggles of our people," I countered. "Back before you were born. I know of it firsthand."

The woman scowled at me and smirked, the

look on her face that of a person responding to what she perceived to be a total wisecrack.

Then she rose to her feet again. "How do you know firsthand? Because you read it in some history book? You saw something about African-American history on—"

"Because I was there!" I said angrily and glared at her.

The room was filled with gasps followed by a momentary silence. The woman's face twisted into a pucker of both disgust and disbelief. "You couldn't have possibly been *there*," she quickly shot back. Suddenly, the mayor's aide interjected, "We're getting off track here, folks. We've got roughly ten minutes before the forum is concluded. The mayor will be taking no further questions tonight."

The church erupted in boos and shouting. A number of people held up large handwritten signs in protest. I began to leave the pulpit as Marcus met me by the sidewall. We walked back to where Mama, Ariel, her parents, and Mama D. had been sitting.

Ariel's father stood up as if he had seen and heard enough. "I think we should be on our way home if we're smart. Things are turning ugly, and this group is like a powder keg ready to explode."

"Okay. I'll meet you guys in the parking lot. I see someone I need to talk to," I said.

I trudged toward the left side of the room to see Boogie, the community activist and dancer I'd met on the South Side. When I got in front of him, he smiled.

"I like how you stood up for yourself up there, Lula. And despite the haters and the naysayers, don't ever get discouraged. You know the saying … a journey of a thousand miles begins with a single step." Boogie suddenly put his hand on my shoulder and guided me closer as he leaned on his cane with his other hand. "But I want to caution you to be careful and keep a low profile," he went on.

"Why?" I asked curiously.

Boogie signaled for me to follow him as he started toward the church's side entrance, which led to the parking lot. He stopped just shy of the doorway. "Let me give you a word of advice, my sister. We've had a number of community activists brutally murdered in this city. Most of the cases are still unsolved. I don't know if it's the gangs, the drug dealers or someone else. But somebody sees them as a threat." Boogie jerked his chin.

"Now, you see that guy near the back of the room with the screen-printed T-shirt and dreads, skin ink up and down his arms? He's a known gang member. That I know for a fact. And he's probably here gathering information to go back and tell his crew about our efforts. I don't want anything happening to you. I thought about that after I met you and your mother over on Halsted." Boogie paused for a moment, took in a breath and then shook his head.

"These are some wicked times we're living in. A lot different than when I was your age. We've already lost some innocent young people to this crazy violence. All I'm saying is … just watch your back."

I nodded. "Okay, I will. And I'll keep in touch."

Boogie extended his hand, and we shook before I slid past several cops and a group of men who looked like aldermen, politicians, or possibly clergy. Once I'd made it outside, a harsh reality washed over me. I started to wonder about this life I'd found myself in. While other young women were out partying, traveling, basically enjoying their most productive years, here I was attempting to fill shoes that might have been meant for someone more courageous, more daring.

But God had put me right where I was for a purpose. Perhaps Mama and I would be the living link from the past to the present to help educate this lost generation. A generation that, in large part, had become morally bankrupt. A generation being duped daily by an evil adversary with a lot of help on this place called earth.

CHAPTER 7

ON A BEAUTIFUL AND calm summer night, my best friend Ariel and her parents invited Mama and me over for a Friday night fish fry at their condominium in Hyde Park. Mama had not spent much time with the Evanses—hadn't spent much time with anyone besides myself, actually.

In my humble opinion, Mama still needed to improve her social skills and how she was going to interact with others in this century, especially white people. Mama and I arrived at the building at a quarter to seven. As I exited my Nissan and opened the door for her, I turned and noted the building's exterior. It instantly brought back memories of my being transported to Fifty-Third Street, homeless and in shock, before being discovered by Ariel.

I leaned over and helped Mama from the car.

She'd been experiencing recurring back pain for several weeks now and needed assistance whenever standing. I was sure that whatever was ailing her must've stemmed from those brutal twelve-hour days laboring on the Mansfield Plantation in the scorching heat.

"We're going to have to get you to a doctor," I told her.

Mama shook her head. "Never needed no doctor pickin' cotton," she muttered.

"Because you didn't have a choice. You didn't have access to one," I replied.

Mama seemed to have become increasingly defiant. I found this especially true now that she no longer answered to white folks, nor their children. I gently escorted her into the building and halfway down the hall, and then saw her eyes go wide as soon as we stopped in front of the bank of elevators.

I chuckled, remembering how I'd had the same fearful reaction when Ariel had first brought me here. I pushed the up arrow and watched the white button illuminate.

"Lula, what are we doing? Where are we going?" Mama asked, unsettled.

"It's okay, Mama. I was scared just like you.

This elevator will take us to the floor where the Evanses live. Trust me. You'll be all right!"

Mama reached out her right hand, holding on to the side of the elevator, then slowly stuck her right foot inside before following with the left. A few seconds later, which I imagined had seemed like an eternity to Mama, we arrived on the Evans's floor.

Ariel walked out of the condo to greet us as soon as we stepped off the elevator.

"Well, I'm glad you all could make it this evening. My mom and dad are cooking walleye he caught in Wisconsin. We're also having hush puppies, coleslaw, and hand-cut French fries. Come on in."

I was happy to see Ariel being her usual giddy self. I assumed that she was angry with neither her parents nor her boyfriend.

Mama and I walked inside. Off to our right was the sound of cooking oil crackling in the kitchen. Immediately I looked to my left at the room I had shared with Ariel. It was funny how things some-times worked. Because I vividly remembered lying there in bed at night, praying that somehow God would reunite us. And now here we were, Mama and me, standing side by side in this very place.

Mama, looking around at the aesthetics of the

condo, must have let her mind wander, because at first she heard neither Mr. Evans nor Mrs. Evans when they greeted us.

Suddenly, she jerked herself out of from her thoughts. "Oh, sorry, ma'am. Pleased to see you again," Mama said, extending her hand.

"Nice to see you as well, Ella Mae. Especially being under normal circumstances."

We all walked into the living room and sat on the sofa. Ariel's mother, Patty, then stood up and announced, "Dinner will be up shortly. In the meantime, I've got something I'd like to show your mother, Lula." Patty calmly trudged into the bedroom and returned seconds later with her and her husband's large and expensive-looking digital camera. She sat on the couch next to Mama, pushed a button to turn on the camera's LCD screen, and then started scrolling through various images.

"These are some shots we took of Lula at the graduation, standing next to the mayor of Chicago," she said beaming. "And then here she is on the jumbo screen. And here she is waving to the crowd. We're talking tens of thousands, Ella Mae, all screaming at the top of their lungs at Soldier Field. It was a total *madhouse*!"

Mama looked at the parade of pictures and smiled graciously. "I'm so proud of my baby girl," she said, then lifted her gaze to focus her attention on the Evanses. "I also want to thank you for everything you've done for her. Taking her off the street and providing a home for her, helping her, you and your daughter, when no one else would."

Mama then rose from the couch, walked around the cocktail table situated in the middle of the floor and gave Randy and Ariel a heartfelt hug. Ariel and her mother then brought out folding dinner trays before we all went into the kitchen, put food on our plates and then headed back to the living room.

After dinner, and since I was driving, Ariel's father poured a glass of nonalcoholic sparkling wine for everyone. I quickly figured that he didn't want to be responsible for starting any bad habits. He stood in the middle of the room like a baseball coach in the dugout after winning the pennant and raised his glass. "Here's a toast to the Darling family. May you ladies find health, happiness, and prosperity for the rest of your lives. *And no more instances of time travel!*"

"I'll toast to that," I said as we all clinked glasses.

As Mama sipped the bubbly drink from her glass, her gaze suddenly zeroed in on a photograph of Ariel's grandmother, which sat on an end table next to the sofa.

"That's my mother, Ella Mae. She passed away last year from cirrhosis. Another reason why we don't drink much around here anymore." Patty shook her head. "Whether due to addiction, suicide, or sickness, our family seems to be getting smaller and smaller," she said.

"I'm sorry to hear that. Sorry for your loss," Mama said, crestfallen. "But at least you all have some extended family left. All I have is my Lula."

Hearing Mama deliver that line, almost immediately, my mind conjured the day Randy had come home excited after he'd verified that I was telling the truth about my past existence. He'd mentioned some website where he had seen Mama's name on some kind of roll for documented slaves. That was definitely worth looking into, I thought.

I wasn't sure if this was the right moment. But with a burning desire to know more, I put my fears aside and summoned the courage to ask him about it. "Mr. Evans, do you remember the website you visited where you saw my mother's name listed as a slave in Natchez?"

Randy nodded. "Yeah. Sure, I remember it."

"Well, what if there was a listing of family

members of slaves? Even if they were sold off and living on some other plantation?" I said.

Randy shrugged. "Well, I guess it would be great to know from a historical standpoint. Knowing who else in your extended family had been a slave. Is that what you mean?"

"More than that," I replied. "I'm thinking that whatever relatives we had back then may have some descendants somewhere alive today. That would make them family, correct?"

Randy folded his arms and looked at me. "All right, Lula. Tell you what, I'll go in the bedroom and get my laptop. I still have that website book-marked as one of my favorites. We'll see what we can find, ladies. As my grandfather used to say when I was a kid … nothing beats a failure but a try."

Ariel's father went into his bedroom and returned several minutes later with his gray MacBook Air. He plugged its power cord into a nearby outlet, then booted up the computer on top of the cocktail table. Mama and I quickly went to the other side of the room to watch as the whole process unfolded. Although I had gotten used to modern technology over time, its benefits and potential drawbacks, Mama was still pretty much in awe of the capabilities.

"Now here's the website," he said. I watched him type Mama's name into the search box near the top of the page. Grasping my knees with my hands for balance, I leaned over the table to take a closer look. Seconds later, several results appeared, showing a possible relative by the name of Hattie Gatlin. A paragraph-long bio stated that she had been a slave in Adams County and had been given the name of her slave owner. Not much else was given. But there had to be a reason why she was linked to Mama's name.

"Does that name ring a bell, Ella Mae?" Ariel's father asked.

Mama shook her head. "No, that name don't ring a bell. I didn't know her," she sighed. "Don't even know much about my parents. We were separated at birth and I wouldn't even know them if I sat next to them in church on Sunday mornings."

Randy turned from looking at Mama. "Okay, let's try something else." He pulled up another website and entered Hattie Gatlin's name, where she was from, her place of birth. A list of possible relatives appeared, some as nearby as Gary, Indiana, which was just minutes away, across state lines.

He then looked up from his laptop computer.

"If you both want to go through this, you can try to contact some of these people. Maybe reach out on Facebook and explain the situation. But I'd be careful about giving away too much info about your past. Now that the Feds know about you both, believe me, they won't be too far behind.

"Your mere *existence* … puts you squarely in the rank of classified information."

Mama and I exchanged a glance. Finding out if we had other relatives out there was definitely worth whatever risks might follow. Perhaps others had taken their families for granted, but when you considered our harrowing journey to the forefront of freedom and everything we'd had to endure, for us, family was everything.

CHAPTER 8

In the following days, I found a young woman online who matched the details of the search we'd done at Ariel's house. The young lady's name was Shantay Gatlin, and she lived in the small town of Gary, Indiana, which is only about a thirty-minute drive from the South Side of Chicago.

I explained to her our connection to Hattie Gatlin, who Shantay had acknowledged was her great-grandmother and also an original native of Mississippi. At first, and not at all surprisingly, Shantay firmly rejected our offer to meet in person. I wholeheartedly understood her reluctance, especially when a stranger contacted you out of nowhere online and claimed to be your relative. But remembering the pearls of wisdom which Ariel's dad had shared during dinner at their condo

—"nothing beats a failure but a try"—I figured we had nothing to lose, but possibly an extended family to gain. So I persisted, and after eventually texting Shantay a picture of Mama and me for the sake of familiarity, she agreed to meet with us the following Saturday.

Mama and I were not banking on the fact that these people would surely turn out to be of kin, but still, we stayed upbeat and hoped for a positive outcome. With all that was going on in the world, we had absolutely no idea what we could possibly be getting ourselves into. In a nutshell, we wanted to go into this with realistic expectations, but also with an abundance of caution. Hence, one of the reasons for us going during the daylight hour.

We started out the morning having breakfast at a bustling café in Bronzeville. It was the first time that Mama had actually been inside of a restaurant outside of Marlene Baker's place on Chicago Avenue. From chicken and waffles to catfish and cornbread, Mama wanted to try just about everything on the menu. After the waitress had brought out our food, we'd been so busy eating, we hadn't had much time to talk about anything. We sampled food from each other's plates, me tasting Mama's fried chicken, her tasting my catfish.

People seated nearby just stared at us and whispered.

When we finally finished, the waitress brought our check. She looked at our empty plates and smiled. "You ladies must have really been hungry." But she had no idea; not only had we left my apartment starving, but this had also been the most food that two former slaves had eaten in their entire lives.

From there we got in my car and headed south on the Dan Ryan Expressway and then east on I-80. We exited the highway on our right and, using GPS tracking on my cell phone, we pulled in front of the two-story white frame house within ten minutes.

Mama and I sat in the car for several moments, observing the house like detectives staking out a potential crime scene. There was a litter of toys in the front yard, and a crumbling sidewalk with bare patches of lawn on either side. We got out of the car, stepped around a plastic yellow school bus, a LEGO set, and a musical rhymes book, which had been left on the pavement. Then we walked up the stairs of the concrete porch. Before I could ring the doorbell, a little girl wearing a cute sweater-and-jeans outfit struggled to pull the door open over thick brown carpet.

"Hi, little princess, my name is Lula, and this is

my mother, Ella Mae. We're here to see Shantay, is she here?"

The girl, who looked to be about five or six, just stared at us, wide-eyed and curious. Then she turned on her heel and yelled at the top of her lungs, "Maaamaaa, they here to see you!"

Cocking my head to the left, I could partially see inside, and I saw several young men in the living room playing video games. Several others were further back in what looked like the kitchen. A few seconds later, a young woman carrying another toddler came to the door.

"You Lula?"

I nodded. "Yes, and this is my mother, Ella Mae."

The young lady quickly studied us from head to toe and then opened the screen door to let us inside. "I'm Shantay. Come on in."

By most standards, she was fairly attractive and a shade lighter than the picture of her I had seen online. Shantay was dressed in a low-cut top bearing most of her cleavage and sashayed when she walked in front of us.

"This is who I was telling y'all about. They say they kin to Great-Grandmamma Hattie," she announced to the three twenty-something men sprawled out across the living room floor. "Come on back to the kitchen."

Mama and I followed Shantay into the kitchen. The three men in the living room paused their game and then clomped into the room behind us. The first thing I noticed was their sagging pants, their heavily tatted arms hanging out of wife beaters, their snickering. Me, Shantay and Mama pulled out wooden chairs and sat at a small oval table the color of walnut.

"So how do y'all know my great-grandmamma?" one of the young men asked. He was slightly muscular, slim, with a strip of peach fuzz over his upper lip and his hair in dreads.

"My mother and I are from Natchez, Mississippi. And we found a website that lists a person's potential relatives based on information submitted. That website listed your great-grandmother, Hattie, as potential kin to my mother here, Ella Mae."

"How we know you all telling the truth? Anybody can say anything. You don't look nothing like her to me," said Shantay.

"We're telling you all the truth. See, my mother and I have no one else to call family. It's just the two of us left. That's why we're searching to see if we have kin alive somewhere."

"You all have a picture of your great-grand-mother, Hattie?" Mama asked.

Shantay shrugged and shook her head as she steadily bounced the toddler on her knee. "I don't know where it is. But right now we need to get to the bottom of this. There are a lot of scams going on out here. We don't know who you people are, just showing up out of the blue," she said, her voice rising. Two of the three young men looked on from standing against the wall, snickering.

Suddenly Mama stood up. I think we could both see where this was heading, and it certainly wasn't in a good place. "We didn't mean you any harm, and didn't come here with no bad intentions. We're sorry to have taken up your time this Saturday morning. We might as well just head back to Chicago," said Mama. I looked at my mother, and in a unified move, we pushed back from the table to get on our feet.

Shantay quickly put her free hand up. "Hold up, I—"

"What in God's name is going on out here?" yelled an old man in a motorized wheelchair. He had seemingly appeared out of nowhere and maneuvered into the kitchen. He was as dark as waterlogged plantation dirt, with white hair and a white beard to match. He was exceedingly thin and wore a red-and-black flannel robe over gray plaid pajamas. His voice was raspy and low. "I'm in the room watching television, then hear all this yappin' and commotion. Who are these people?" he asked, squinting his eyes at us.

"They claim they kin to Great-Grandmamma Hattie," Shantay muttered.

I glanced at Mama and wondered just what on earth had we gotten ourselves into. At this point, I could not wait to leave and head home. Shantay and the young men left the room. The old man toggled a switch on his wheelchair and then rolled over to the edge of the kitchen table. "Joe Gatlin," he said, extending his hand. "You'll have to excuse my family here. That is my niece, and those are my nephews, and they're very protective of me. I can't say I blame them. There's a lot of scam artists trying to take advantage of seniors nowadays. Please … sit down. How can I help you ladies?"

Mama and I slowly settled back in our seats. "We did some research and found Hattie's name linked to my mother's on an ancestral website, which means they could be some kin," I said.

"Where you from, and what's your last name?" Joe asked.

"Natchez, Mississippi. The last name is Darling," Mama replied. "This is my daughter, Lula, and I'm Ella Mae."

Joe cracked a smile. "Well, Hattie *was* born in Mississippi, a slave up until the time they all got their freedom. Then she moved up North, lived the rest of her days in Louisville, Kentucky. She had always been proud to live in the same place where the champ, Muhammad Ali, had called home. I remember staying at her house for several weeks each summer when I was a boy."

Joe Gatlin leaned forward, getting a good look at Mama. "You share some of the same features as Hattie. The both of you have high cheekbones. Not everyone has those."

"You got any pictures of her?" Mama asked curiously.

Joe nodded. "I think I may have a few. Let me see what I can scramble up."

He swiveled his wheelchair around, went into what was apparently his bedroom and returned with a heavily worn beige photo album. He set it on top of the table and started flipping the pages. Mama and I leaned forward to take a closer look.

"This was a picture taken of her and her husband, Paul, right after their wedding. He died a

long time before she did. Had a heart attack. And
when word got out about his death, no one hardly
even noticed. You wanna know why?"

"Why?" asked Mama.

"Because he was a *rotten* something. Man, he
used to whup Hattie something fierce. He was
insanely jealous and controlling."

I shook my head. "No man should ever beat or
put his hands on a woman." God knows I'd seen
some beatings growing up, including women. I
remembered the time when Hartley Mansfield had
raised his hand, preparing to slap Mama after he
thought she'd mumbled something smart under her
breath. This had occurred on the steps of the big
house not long after my father had died. Fortunately, Martha Mansfield had been standing nearby
and, seeing what was about to transpire, had lunged
forward to grab his arm before he could deliver
that blow.

"I agree, no man should ever hit a woman," Joe
replied. "But Paul was guilty of all of that
nonsense. And if that wasn't bad enough, he was
also accused of molesting his own daughters. A sick
man he was. If you want to even call him a man.
All that malarkey continued until Hattie's two eldest
sons gave him a taste of his own medicine. They

beat that man senseless. Put him in the hospital in a coma for two months. After he died, Hattie, understandably, went back to using her maiden name again."

Joe continued to slowly turn the pages. "These are other family members. Some have passed on. Some we haven't been in contact with." Then Joe paused for a moment and let out what seemed like a frustrated breath. "Seems like everyone is in their own little world nowadays. That's why I don't do all that texting and email stuff like you young people. I'm old-school. I have to communicate just like what we're doing now. For me, it's more personal."

He looked at me and smiled. Then he turned almost to the end of the album. There were miscellaneous pieces of paper, what looked like a high school diploma, a marriage certificate, several mementos and trinkets, all barely kept in place behind worn plastic covering.

"What's that?" I asked, gazing at a faded, brown-tinted piece of paper. It looked like an old newspaper article. Joe pulled the clipping out from behind a handwritten biblical verse: Isaiah 41:10. He turned it toward Mama and me so that we could see it up close.

"My eyes are bad now. Ain't worth a damn

anymore. See if you can read that for me, please. Tell me what it says, sweetheart."

I looked more closely and saw that it was an advertisement—cotton and rice Negroes for sale in Adams County, the same county where Mama, Hattie, and I had resided. In smaller print were the names of each alleged family member offered up for sale. I lowered my gaze to read the names on each line and then pointed, my adrenaline rising. "Look at that, Mama."

My mother instantly brightened. "Ella Mae," she murmured upon seeing her name.

"And what does it say beneath that?" I said.

Mama ran a finger under the next listing. "Hattie!" she exclaimed.

I smiled, now thinking this had all been worth it. "I guess that kind of confirms it."

Joe tilted his head to one side with a look somewhere between slightly annoyed and puzzled. "What does that confirm? You had a great-grandmother named Ella Mae too?"

"Yes," Mama told him. "It was said that she worked on another plantation before being auctioned off to the Mansfields in Adams County," she went on.

"Outside of DNA testing, which I imagine is

not an option at this point in time, I guess it's safe to assume that we're actually related, Mr. Gatlin," I added.

Joe looked at me and then at Mama. He looked perplexed for several seconds before finally managing a smile.

"Well, all this has got my head spinning, I ain't gonna lie. But, anyhow ... welcome to the family," he said, reaching out to embrace us from his wheel-chair. "I look forward to inviting you both to our next big family event. I gotta caution you, though," Joe said, shaking his head, "once you see everything that goes on with this dysfunctional bunch, you might regret you ever came here. Don't say I didn't warn you!"

Mama and I laughed heartily at Joe's brutal honesty.

"They're a handful, especially for an old man like me. But I did what any noble brother should do under the circumstances. I took them all in when my sister died of cervical cancer," Joe explained.

"Sorry for your loss," Mama and I said in unison.

"Thank you. But, no, it's okay. It's been about fourteen years now last November and, well, time's got a way of healing all wounds, as they say," Joe added, nodding his head.

He continued. "Got one up there in the living room on house arrest for stealing out of a convenience store. I've also gotta keep a watchful eye on my niece's daughter, Takira, who's got a bad habit of leaving out of the house unsupervised and wandering off down the street, exploring the neighborhood. Last time she did that, we found her all the way over on the next block," Joe said, pointing toward the front of the house.

"I've told Shantay time and time again to keep an eye on her daughter. But do you think she listens? Heck no."

"I hope she starts to listen. There are a lot of young black girls now missing in Washington, D.C., and other parts of the country. And the problem is not getting the attention it so rightfully deserves," I responded.

"That's why I'm all about family. Keeping family first. We got to stick together and look out for one another. Something we used to do a lot better compared to what we're doing today," Joe said enthusiastically.

"You ever been married, had a wife to call your own, Joe?" Mama asked.

Joe tilted his head to one side again and smiled. "Well, I *was* married at one time in my life. Her name was Ruby Brown. She was originally from the great state of Georgia. Once we fell in love—I couldn't resist giving her the nickname of Sweet Georgia Brown. I did everything I could for that woman, to make her happy and to provide a good life for her. I owned a bar at the time, and by my estimation, we had a good life.

"However, she wasn't satisfied. She ended up running off with some big-time drug dealer she'd met on the West Side of Chicago. The stress of the marriage damn near killed me. I lost the bar, incurred a ton of debt and eventually lost my house. My sister suggested I come live with her to get on my feet, and then she passed away.

"Ruby was living high on the hog. She used to parade around town in her fur coats and big silver Mercedes. To this day I still remember the details of when the marriage ended. I was at the bar one morning helping a liquor delivery driver bring in some inventory. That was the day she packed up to leave, which I would not have known anything about had it not been for my neighbor alerting me. He called me while I was at the bar and told me that she was moving out. He witnessed it firsthand while looking out his living room window.

"Immediately, I left the bar and hurried home to see her standing in our living room, clutching a suitcase in one hand and a duffel bag full of shoes in the other. For the life of me, I couldn't understand it. So I stood in the doorway and asked her why? I just wanted to make sense of it all.

"Her last and exact words to me were: 'I want more, Joe. I want to live a life that you're not capable of giving me. Now, if you'll excuse yourself from blocking the door so that I can leave, I'd appreciate it. I got livin' to do!'"

Joe let out a deep breath. "She was a real floozy. Sometimes you never really know who that person is sleeping beside you in bed at night. Who knows? Maybe I'll give marriage another try someday should the right woman come along. But I ain't holding my breath."

Joe then called Shantay and her brothers back into the kitchen for an opportunity to get to know us and bond like family. From what little I could ascertain about Shantay and her siblings in the short time that Mama and I had been here, I felt that perhaps there was something positive I could bring to each and every one of their lives. And I was just as certain that there were things Mama and I could learn and benefit from by being a part of this union, too.

Shantay picked up her toddler from the floor after seeing him trying to open up a cabinet door. "Uncle Joe, did you tell them about your younger days, when you were considered gangsta?" she said and smiled.

Joe turned toward Mama and me. "What she's referring to is my past involvement with the Black Panthers. Surely you ladies must be familiar with their story and their effort to help black people?"

Mama and I exchanged glances. "No," I said, my curiosity piqued. "But I'd like to know more."

"Well, I used to assist them. The Panthers were an organization that did good in the community, looking out for the interests of black people. They also had an undeserved reputation for being a radical antiestablishment group. But that wasn't the case at all. They would give out free breakfasts for children and helped patrol black neighborhoods to ward off police brutality. In my opinion, today, we lack the leaders with the kind of backbone that our civil rights icons had during the sixties."

Joe leaned forward. "Today, due mostly to social engineering, many of our inner cities are crime-ridden, drug-infested death traps. Real leadership in our communities have been eliminated, and the dumping of drugs and weapons on our streets has led to what we have become.

"It's simple arithmetic, really. Destruction of communities leads to destructive people. Easy access to liquor and drugs in hopeless areas leads to hopeless people. Limited access to good-quality, nutritious food and health care leads to sick and dying people. Now, how many quality grocery stores do you see in areas where we live?"

I shook my head. "Not many," I replied.

Joe nodded. "That's correct. You mostly see only fast-food options," he said. "The bottom line is, we got to wake up and get it together."

I was thankful that I had the opportunity to hear more about the history that I'd missed. Skipping over a century of time had left a cultural void that Mama and I were still trying to fill, or at least make some kind of sense of. This brief glimpse of Joe Gatlin's perspective gave me even more motivation to learn about the Black Panthers and many of the events throughout history that I knew nothing about.

For roughly forty-five minutes, we shared our stories, dreams, and present-day life experiences. I even found out that Shantay's brother, Julius, who they affectionately referred to as Ju Ju, was an aspiring rapper, not unlike Marcus was when he'd first started, rhyming for dollars on the streets of downtown Chicago. I told Ju Ju about Marcus and his rise to prominence in the music business, and promised him that I would introduce them as soon as possible.

Mama and I vowed to keep in touch with the Gatlins and assured them that we looked forward to meeting the rest of the extended family at their next gathering. After that, we said goodbye, then got in our car and headed back to the South Side.

CHAPTER 9

AFTER MANY MONTHS of being homebound and probably suffering immensely from cabin fever, my mother was finally prepared to start looking for a job. After several days of me spreading the word, Marlene Baker, the loving woman with a heart of gold who'd found Mama lying on the street on Chicago Avenue, offered my mother a job in her restaurant performing a number of duties: washing dishes, cleaning and waiting on tables.

It was ten minutes to eight. I had taken a half-day off from work, and my evening class at DePaul didn't start until 5 p.m. Mama was dressed in her favorite white blouse and a pair of khakis and was wearing her hair all-natural and parted on one side. I knew that Mrs. Baker's restaurant opened promptly at nine. And I also knew that we were going to have to move through traffic like a scalded squirrel just to get there on time. I had been extremely grateful for everything that Marlene had done—helping Mama find shelter, and also finding me.

We arrived on Chicago Avenue a few minutes before Mama was to start her shift. I had been nervous during the whole thirty-minute trek from home, constantly checking my watch, desperately trying to make it here without killing us both in the process. With it being her first day on the job, I definitely wanted my mother to make a good impression. I knew how hard jobs were to find in this economy and didn't want Marlene to think that we had taken her kind gesture for granted. Eventually, after weaving through traffic for several minutes, we found an hourly lot around the corner, where we parked and then headed toward the restaurant.

The streets were congested with vehicles, buses, and delivery trucks. There were large pockets of pedestrians along the sidewalk. And on the corner, a small group of people held signs protesting the latest policies on immigration. Once in front of the restaurant, I pulled open the glass door to Marlene's place. There was smooth jazz playing through some speakers mounted on the ceiling. And Marlene was

busy talking on the phone as she counted money—
just before sliding a stack of crisp bills into the
register.

Mama and I took a seat at one of the nearby
tables as I admired the décor. It didn't take a genius
to know that Mrs. Marlene had done quite well for
herself—a black woman who owned her own
successful business, especially down in this part of
the city. From across the room, Marlene nodded to
acknowledge our coming in. Then she ended her
call, smiled, and walked over to greet us.

"Ella Mae, Lula, good to see you all again. I
really had to push myself to get in here on time
after the busy weekend I had. After a rather long
courtship with her live-in fiancé, my niece, Twyla,
finally got married. Would you like to see a short
clip of the wedding?"

Mama and I both nodded at Marlene's generosity. I had always imagined that weddings were
something special, even under not-so-ideal circumstances like back in nineteenth-century Natchez.
Marriage was something I imagined most young
girls and women had aspired to, like when a young
princess finally meets her Prince Charming.

Marlene took something out of her purse from
behind the bar and then hurried toward us, her

breathing labored. "I have some footage I took with my iPhone. This is the start of the ceremony." Mama and I stared as two young black girls danced and twirled in front of a pulpit as gospel music swelled in the background. They were dressed in white ballerina outfits and moved about the room in synchronized rhythms.

"What are they doing?" I asked.

"They're called praise dancers. Some brides and grooms use them to give the wedding a religious aspect." Marlene pointed at her cell phone's screen. "Now this is where everyone stood up, and my niece walked down the aisle. That's her father beside her. He was the one who gave her away."

"She looks so lovely and elegant," Mama said, brightening.

Marlene nodded. "She really went all out for the occasion, that's for sure. She spent goo-gobs of money just on that dress alone!"

We watched as Marlene's niece and her husband exchanged their vows, and as he placed the ring on her finger. I didn't know the bride, of course, but felt a surge of happiness rise within and hoped that one day that would be me, standing there, radiant, saying "I do."

Marlene tapped her phone to stop the video

and then looked at Mama. "So, Ella Mae, you ready to start your first paying job?" She grinned broadly with a smile that I imagined could melt the heart of the world's most soulless person.

"Yes, ma'am. Ready as I'm ever going to be," Mama replied.

"Good, 'cause you're all the help I have until around ten o'clock. We usually have a few customers come in early. But the majority of our business is not until lunchtime. I'm going to have you work out on the floor until then. You can start by taking drink orders, and I'll handle the rest."

Marlene grabbed a menu off a nearby table and showed Mama the beverage selection. It consisted of coffee, including the iced variety, flavored teas, sodas, and alcoholic drinks, including beers from several local breweries, although Marlene informed Mama that she herself would handle any alcohol requests until more help arrived. Then she took Mama behind the bar and showed her how to fill orders and where the coffeemaker and inventory of drinks and utensils were located.

Having a few hours of downtime, I pulled out my cell phone and checked to see if I had any messages. While checking its screen, I heard the door of the restaurant swing open. I turned to my left and saw a man come through the doorway with a laptop in hand. He darted his eyes throughout the restaurant and then sat at an empty table next to where I was seated.

He was a tall white man with auburn hair, dressed in a dark blue suit and wearing sunglasses. He looked totally Ivy League. Marlene apparently saw him come through the door and pointed in his direction, instructing Mama to come and take his order. Mama smoothed out several small wrinkles in her shirt, then came from around the bar with a small pad and pencil, eager to get started.

"Good morning, sir. What can I get for you today?"

The man opened his laptop and began typing. "I'll have a hot coffee, no cream, two packs of sugar." He barely looked away from the keyboard as he gave his order. Mama then hurried around the bar, grabbed a mug and poured some coffee into it. Marlene had disappeared somewhere into the back of the restaurant, possibly to handle another phone call.

Mama brought the cup and two packets of sugar to the table. The man lifted the cup and took a sip from the mug; immediately, his face contorted into an expression of disgust. "Why, this is horrible!" he said. "It tastes like something out of a damn sewer. Make it over," he protested.

He abruptly pushed the cup near the edge of the table. He also had what sounded to me like a heavy British accent. Perhaps he had just relocated to this side of the pond. Or perhaps he was simply in a bad mood. Whatever the case, my instincts took over, and I felt like I had to say something.

"It's her first day on the job. If you'd like, I'm sure she can make the coffee over, sir."

He looked at his watch. "That won't be necessary. I've only got fifteen minutes to spare. All I wanted was a cup of coffee and you people can't even do that right!"

"Excuse me?" I said.

"You heard me. I meant what I said and make no apologies for it." He leaned forward and then smiled sarcastically. "Now what are you going to do about it, huh? Nothing, I suppose. You're probably much better off working in the ghetto parts of town, yes?"

Both Mama and I drew close to him. My heart was racing wildly. My pulse began to hammer.

"Don't you talk to my daughter that way!" Mama scolded, pointing a finger at him.

Then he pushed her.

Mama staggered backward. Then she dashed to the bar to grab a broom as I aggressively shoved him back into the table. About that time, Marlene had returned from the back of the restaurant. She looked flabbergasted.

"What's going on?" she blurted.

"Your employees assaulted me! Besides your bad coffee, you've got piss-poor service here. You have no idea who you're dealing with. I'll have this bloody place shut down!" he hissed.

Marlene looked at Mama and then at me. I could tell that Marlene had been temporarily at a loss for words, waiting for some kind of explanation. "Mama was nothing but nice to him. He didn't like his coffee and then started insulting us, telling us to go back to the ghetto," I said.

Marlene looked the man squarely in his face. "Leave, or I'm calling the police."

He walked closer to Marlene—invading her personal space. He plumbed his hands into his pants pocket. "Call the police? Who do you think they're going to believe, huh? I'll simply wait here for them to come so I can file charges of assault and battery."

Marlene turned and pointed toward small black surveillance cameras that were mounted at opposite ends of the restaurant. "Everything that happened is on that tape. And the tape don't lie," she said. Then she went and picked up the phone, which had been lying on top of the bar, and dialed 911, enraged. This was the first time I'd ever seen her not smiling. The man glared at the three of us before he went back to the table where he'd been sitting. He grabbed his laptop, slammed it shut and immediately headed for the door, where he disappeared back into the world.

CHAPTER 10

AFTER SELLING hundreds of thousands of copies of his debut song on the Internet, Marcus had been selected to present a Grammy onstage to one of his mentors, a hugely successful Chicago-based rap music performer and philanthropist. It had been inspiring seeing Marcus ascend to such heights, and I was completely thrilled to see his dream of "making it" finally come to fruition.

Not only had he managed to do all of this without being signed to a major record label, but he'd also been able to amass a following simply on the popularity of his videos trending on YouTube. Now that a significant amount of money had started to come in, all Marcus ever talked about was the chance to finally move Mama D. out of her home, away from the madness of "the hood," and into some different surroundings.

He had also found within his heart a desire to give something back to the community. He planned to open a community center where young people could learn marketable skills as an alternative to making unwise choices in the streets. He wanted them to have opportunities just like he'd had. He was tired of seeing kids succumb to violence, or get sent to prison—kids with a promising future. I was happy he wanted to pay it forward, and I, for one, envisioned ... how much additional progress could be made if more pro athletes, entertainers, and anyone of higher means had the empathy and compassion to follow suit.

Marcus entered the backstage dressing area here at the Staples Center, and everyone present immediately took notice. He'd always had that commanding presence and engaging smile that drew you in, putting you at ease, even if you were having a bad day. He had invited me, Ariel, and her boyfriend, Tommy, to share in the celebration. Marcus spent several minutes talking to some industry bigwigs, then came over and stood in front of me, smoothing the lapels of his jacket with the palms of his hands.

"How do I look? I'll be going onstage in about fifteen minutes. And I'm nervous as all get-out. This is the most people I've ever been in front of in my *entire life*," Marcus said over slightly nervous breath.

"You look good. Just don't overthink it. I know you'll do just fine," I told him and smiled.

Tommy got up from sitting next to Ariel and smiled too. He stood a little over six feet, slim, with a shaved head, boyishly charming good looks, and a diamond sparkling in his left ear. He looked like he could have easily fit in with one of those '90s boy bands that Ariel kept photos of and had proudly displayed on her bedroom wall in the past.

Tommy walked over to Marcus and gave him a huge congratulatory hug. Tommy looked proud, almost like a parent of a kid who'd graduated with honors and was off to some Ivy League college somewhere on the East Coast. Being with Marcus, I believed, had given Tommy hope. To make better choices in life and to watch the company he kept. He looked proud to be a part of his friend's success and over-the-hills happy to be here amid the glitz and glamour, celebrities and paparazzi, and all things hype, here at this year's Grammys in LA.

"Go out there and do your thing, bro. You've

got this," he said as the two of them continued their embrace.

Marcus nodded and smiled. "Thanks, dude. I'm glad that you and Ariel could make it. We're gonna have some *fun* tonight, believe that."

A woman dressed in a dark pantsuit and wearing a headset came over to us and leaned forward. "Two minutes," she said and pointed toward the dressing room door.

Marcus subsequently bent over and kissed my cheek. "Thanks for being my girl, my best friend, and for supporting me. Remember, after the show, the limo is picking us up curbside and taking us to the after-party, one of many," Marcus said as he darted his gaze between Ariel, Tommy, and me.

Looking at him smiling, I was so proud of him. Although, I feared some of what I'd heard about the music industry—the horror stories of drugged-out celebrities, stars who either overdosed or committed suicide, and didn't want Marcus to fall victim to any of its vices. I wanted him to remain grounded, regardless of how much success and notoriety would come his way in the future. I was sure that Mama D., in all her valuable wisdom, had felt the same. After saying what he needed to say, he quickly left the room to go onstage.

I watched nervously as Marcus gave a brief presentation, then handed the Grammy to the winner of the Best New Artist category. The recipient gave his acceptance speech and then began to exit the stage. But Marcus remained standing there. I leaned over to focus in on the monitor in the dressing room, wondering what he'd planned to say next.

Marcus moved forward, closer to the microphone. "Right quick, I just want to say, my girlfriend's name is Lula Darling, and she is going to change the world, y'all! She's starting to do some amazing things to help correct the injustices that we've seen in this country, starting in Chicago! As a matter of fact, and I know I'm gonna catch a lot of flak for this, but I want her to run out for only a few minutes and deliver a brief message!"

After hearing Marcus say what he'd said, I was shocked beyond belief. I shot a quick glance at Ariel and Tommy. "Go! Hurry up! This is your chance to deliver your message to millions!" Ariel called out.

I stood up and walked past several men in suits who looked like part of the show's production crew. They had no clue Marcus was referring to me, and within earshot, I overheard one of them say,

"What's he doing? He can't do this. Who does he think he is, Kanye West?"

Unfazed, I hightailed it across the platform to center stage. My heart was beating a mile a minute, my palms sweaty. Marcus moved away from the microphone for me to talk. I figured I'd have only about five or ten seconds before security would yank me off stage, and possibly even have me arrested for trespassing.

"To the young generation and people of color watching this, I just want to say that, although we've made some progress historically, at the same time, we've lost our cultural pride, respect, and overall—we've become morally bankrupt. We need to raise our standards and our self-esteem. Society is unraveling. The time for a change is now! No more talking. No more marching. It's time we try something new, y'all! Who is with me? Who wants to help change the world?"

The audience broke into raucous applause and cheered. Several rappers from the back of the room ran toward the stage but were blocked in the process. Suddenly instrumental music began playing as a signal that the show needed to stay on schedule. About that time two beefy men came onto the stage, one from each side. I knew they'd come to escort me away, so I saved them the trouble.

Marcus and I calmly walked off, waving and smiling at the audience like we were the president and the first lady taking the final steps of an inaugural dance. As soon as we made it backstage and into the dressing room, a tall, slim, gaunt man holding a clipboard charged inside and pointed his finger at me, and then at Marcus.

"Don't you ever do that again! You two have completely thrown tonight's show off schedule and are this close to being permanently banned from attending any more award shows in the future. Do I make myself perfectly clear?" he growled, squeezing his thumb and index finger close together to illustrate his point.

Marcus walked over to him and boldly entered his personal space. "Yo, man, chill, all right? My girl just had a simple public announcement that only took up a few seconds. It was something the masses needed to hear. It won't happen again, okay?"

The man turned and then stormed out of the dressing room. Afterward, Tommy and Ariel stood and walked over to congratulate us. I could look at their faces and see that they had been really impressed. "Yo, that was dope, dude. The way you two took over the stage and could have cared less about the blowback," Tommy muttered as he gave Marcus a handshake and then a hug.

"Hey, how about a picture?" said Marcus. "All four of us, to capture the moment." Marcus went outside the dressing room, where there was a petite Asian woman talking to someone over her headset. She was nursing a bottle of Fiji water as she walked. "You mind taking a quick snapshot of my friends and me?" Marcus asked.

"Sure. No problem."

Marcus handed her his cell phone, and the four of us huddled close together as she took three consecutive pictures. Then I heard her suddenly mutter into her headset, "I'll be right there."

Marcus glanced at his watch and then looked at the room's monitor, where in several minutes, the Lifetime Achievement Award would be given to some deserving artist. Several minutes later, a trio of young black men came into the dressing room looking for Marcus. They were wearing black tuxedo-styled suits over crushed velvet shirts, and hanging from each of their necks were probably tens of thousands of dollars' worth of either platinum or white gold chains and medallions. They also wore sparkling diamond-encrusted watches and matching rings, which adorned most of the fingers on their heavily tatted hands.

Marcus got up from his seat and immediately embraced them. "Lula, Ariel, Tommy, this gentleman right here is none other than Morris Scott, more famously known as Jay Killa, the executive producer of my debut album, and one of the most successful and respected men in hip-hop."

Jay Killa stepped forward and flashed a kilowatt smile that could seemingly light up half of Hollywood. I had only heard Marcus mention him sporadically but knew that this guy was like a mentor to him and someone whom he looked up to. Jay Killa reached forward and shook each of our hands. He seemed friendly enough, even though his eyes remained hidden behind a pair of expensive-looking black-and-gold shades.

"I'm having one of the sickest, most off-the-chain after-parties in the Hills tonight and would like each one of you to attend as my personal VIP guests. Although this is our first time meeting, if you're with Marcus, well, that's all the guarantee I need to know that you're good people. My limo will be out front in twenty minutes to take you to the party. Oh, and I liked your speech. It took some nerve to get up there and say what you said tonight."

"Thank you," I said and smiled. "I seem to find myself in front of crowds quite a bit lately."

"Well, I look at that as a good thing," Jay Killa replied. "The more people that see you and hear you speak, hopefully, the bigger your following and movement will be."

"That's what I'm hoping will happen. Although I'm not really seeking any personal gain or notoriety, only tangible results."

Jay Killa nodded and then turned on his heels to meet up with his entourage, which consisted of groupies and what looked like either publicists or agents or both. After several more hugs, handshakes, and goodbyes, just as quick as he'd come backstage at the Staples Center to introduce himself, the rap impresario was gone.

Almost as if telepathic-like, I looked over at Ariel and her eyes met my gaze. I knew that we were both of one accord and were now ready to leave. Earlier, she'd complained about her feet hurting from walking in her heels. So by this time, we were ready to kick back and explore whatever the rest of the night had in store. The four of us figured it would take some time to filter through the crowd to get out to Jay Killa's limo, so we gathered our belongings and promptly left the dressing room.

Once we'd ventured out into the cool nighttime air of downtown LA, we trudged along Figueroa Street, past a group of would-be rappers chanting lyrics, some scantily dressed women, people snapping selfies, to where the limousine was waiting. The limo itself was a shining black stretch Hummer. The driver, a squat fifty-something black man, opened the door for us as we got in. There were already a number of people inside, maybe eighteen to twenty by my brief estimation. I imagined that somewhere within the mix, Jay Killa was seated, keeping a low profile, waiting to be transported to a place of extreme decadence.

"Oooh, man, this ride is sick!" Marcus exclaimed. He smiled and gave Tommy a high five.

Of course, I'd never had the opportunity or been fortunate enough to ride inside of a limousine. Immediately I admired its contemporary styling, its custom leather interior, the two flat-screens playing hip-hop videos, the club-style lighting, the bar and music options. The limo pulled away, and after leaving the confines of the Staples Center, we snaked our way through the massive traffic in the heart of downtown LA.

As the vehicle rolled down the street, Marcus talked excitedly over the music that blared through the speakers about when he would be working on and releasing his next record. Tommy and Ariel talked about the realistic possibility of the two of them getting married. I wondered how sincere he was in saying that to my best friend, because I knew that sometimes during a festive occasion or during a celebration, people got caught up in the moment and would say things that they didn't really mean. In between the constant conversation among the four of us, I peered out the tinted window at Tinseltown like a curious child in an enchanted forest.

Eventually, the urban landscape gave way to a sprawling suburb, and we came upon a residential area with tall trees and massive homes. The streets were almost completely dark and relatively quiet compared to what I was used to in Chicago. There were rows and rows of privacy shrubs blocking the gargantuan homes from prying eyes. Most of these mansions sat on huge lots and were elevated from the street on which we were traveling. I looked up at the pitch-dark mountainous terrain and immediately wondered how many celebrities lived here.

"Almost there," the driver blurted, jolting my thoughts.

The limo made several winding turns and then started to climb uphill.

Tommy leaned over and gave Ariel a kiss on the cheek. Then he looked out the window opposite to where he was seated. "Hey, is this, like—where that whole O.J. thing occurred?"

A young twenty-something man who had been sitting directly across from Tommy and Ariel shook his head. "Nah, bro, that was Brentwood."

I had absolutely no idea what they were talking about. "O.J.? You mean like orange juice?" I said. With California's balmy weather, I figured it was safe to assume that whatever they were talking about had to do with the fruit and nothing else. Still, the joke was apparently lost on me.

Everyone in the back half of the limo burst out laughing. They all looked at me as if I had two heads, staring incredulously as if to say: *Really?*

Tommy folded his arms, smiled, and leaned forward awaiting my response. "You're joking, right? Surely you're old enough to know who O.J. Simpson is, Lula. The former pro football player?"

They must have thought that either I was pulling their legs, or just downright clueless when it came to most matters of the world. Before I could shake my head no, Marcus and Ariel quickly came to my rescue. "Of course she knows that O.J. was acquitted of murdering his wife, but is now in prison on unrelated charges." Marcus shook his head and laughed. "Hey, she's tired, okay? It's been a long day. My girl just had a little lapse in judgment, that's all."

Speaking of states, mental lapses, and prison, my mind had been drawn back to Tommy. Ever since I'd known him, he'd been the classic definition of a bad boy. I also knew that at one point he had been on house arrest, and wondered if he actually had the all-clear to be here in California. There were times during the summer when I had stopped by his house with Ariel, only to see a probation officer standing in Tommy's living room, checking on his whereabouts. But all of this was really none of my business, so I mostly stayed out of his and Ariel's relationship.

Marcus and Ariel were the only ones inside of this limo who knew my secret. Ariel, who'd always had trouble keeping secrets, had somehow managed *not* to tell Tommy that Mama and I were time travelers from a distant past.

The vehicle reached the top of the hill and crested in front of a well-lit property where cars were double- and triple-parked leading up to its entrance. Mercedes, Jaguars, several Rolls-Royces and Bentleys. We all got out of the Hummer, and I was immediately taken in by the size and breadth of the house. White, with floor-to-ceiling windows and an architectural-style design, it looked more like a modern office building than a home where someone had actually lived. It reminded me of the homes I'd seen in the numerous *Architectural Digest* magazines that Ariel's mother often kept on her living room cocktail table. Ariel bent over and slid on her shoes, which she had removed during the ride from the Grammys, and everyone followed in a line toward the front of the house.

The door was opened as if someone had been watching us as we approached. We entered and stood inside a large foyer area. Next, a man named Bryce strolled from around a sidewall and greeted us. He smiled, and from his serving tray he offered the women among us strawberry-pineapple mimosas, and then he offered the men sparkling glasses of chilled Moët & Chandon. He motioned us inside to join the party, where people were locked in conversation, laughing, and dancing to the Bruno Mars hit "24K Magic" as it blared throughout the main level.

"Who lives here?" Tommy asked, obviously impressed.

"Some big record company honcho. I believe he's the executive producer of Killa's album and is honoring him tonight in appreciation of his latest album going double platinum," Marcus replied.

With its expensive interior design and impressive square footage, this place looked more like a museum. Ariel and I looked around as the four of us were led into another section of the property. We'd been told it was the only place where there were still some seats available.

The four of us were ushered past several men playing pool in a rec room off to the side. Ariel and I took a seat in what we were told was the great room as Marcus and Tommy went to a patio door observing an outdoor pool and Jacuzzi. Sitting next to Ariel and me appeared to be two tall and somewhat muscular females. Upon closer inspection, and from the width and squareness of their shoulders, I could definitely tell they were transgender.

The music abruptly stopped, and my eyes were drawn back to the center of the room, where there was a rush of people looking to make some type of announcement. A distinguished-looking man, middle-aged, tanned, dressed in a gray designer suit, with a lot of plastic surgery, smiled as someone handed him a cordless microphone. Another man and a woman flanked his side.

"Distinguished guests, I'd like to thank you for coming out to our Grammy after-party tonight in the Hollywood Hills. I promise you I'll keep this short, because I know there's more fun to be had than for you to sit around and hear me talk." The man briefly scanned the room and smiled. "Besides, I do enough of that at work throughout the day. For those of you who don't know by now, my name is Theodore Schrementi, and I am the vice president of Mystère Records. Tonight we are celebrating for two reasons. One, because it is Grammy night. Two, because I wish to publicly congratulate one of Mystère's most successful artists this year, for his going two times platinum. I'm talking about one of the most downloaded rappers today—and my good friend, Jay Killa."

Everyone in the room cheered and clapped as Jay Killa walked to the center of the room to shake Schrementi's hand. There was some slight feedback from the mike and a whine that had everyone covering their ears momentarily. Jay Killa took the microphone, smiled, and briefly cleared his throat.

"Thank you, Theo, for that warm and meaningful introduction. No one in this game is responsible for doing it alone. Any successful artist, you'll find, is going to have a strong and capable team behind them, as is the case here. So, I'd truly and personally like to thank you, sir," Jay Killa said and nodded. "I'd also like to thank the hardworking staff in A&R and promotions, and all the great people at Mystère who are responsible for making all of this happen. And to be honest, quite frankly, I've already set big goals for my next record to do just as well." Jay Killa paused for a moment.

"Now, I don't mean to sound cocky, but I am humbly striving to become the best-selling rapper of all time!" There was an abundance of cheering and catcalls. "I know it's not going to be easy, but like I heard someone say before—I think it was a great man who said it. He said: 'Aim for the moon, and even if you miss you'll be among the stars,'" Jay Killa went on. Then he raised his glass toward the ceiling and proposed a toast. "Here's to another breakout year next year!"

Everyone clapped and whistled as Jay Killa was presented with a framed version of his megaselling CD. He and Schrementi wrapped their arms around each other's shoulders and posed for pictures. Marcus took snapshots of the music business duo with his cell phone. Afterward, Jay Killa stood there for several minutes and shook the hands of various well-wishers. Theodore Schrementi grabbed a glass of wine and walked outside to an infinity pool overlooking what I assumed to be parts of LA, lights glimmering in the distance.

Forty-five minutes later, over thumping techno, Jay Killa announced to Marcus that he was having his own after-party at his hotel suite downtown. Several rooms had been rented, and there was limited space available, he told us. Which meant that not everyone here was invited. But through Marcus's association with the rap star, the four of us were.

After watching a brief fireworks show off the greystone deck behind Schrementi's massive home, we summoned a limo to take us directly to Jay Killa's after set. When we arrived, a crowd had already swelled in the middle of the hotel's lobby. The group was racially diverse, whites, blacks, Latinos. Some of them already appeared to be tipsy. The four of us snaked through the group and took the first bank of elevators up to the ninth floor. I had been both nervous and excited during the entire ride here. We had been told that Jay Killa's eighteen-hundred-dollar-a-night suite was nothing short of amazing, and that no expenses had been spared on either the catered food or the drinks.

We walked down a dimly lit carpeted hallway and stood in front of Jay Killa's room. His assistant removed a key card from his wallet, waved it across the magnetic sensor and allowed everyone to go in. It was eight of us, to be exact. We spilled into the suite, and Ariel and I immediately walked around, stunned.

Marcus wasted no time in bragging about the entire night. "Hey, did I not tell you all how big we do it at Integra? Look at this room. Killa rented out two humongous suites!" he said as he strolled into the bedroom.

"Just how big is this suite?" Tommy asked.

"Over thirteen hundred square feet of pure indulgence," Marcus replied as he poured himself a glass of champagne.

"This is bigger than my parents' condo," Ariel added.

Marcus walked over to an ice bucket atop a mini bar and filled glasses for me, Ariel and Tommy. Then he turned on some music from the room's stereo system. I turned and saw that there were other people filing into the suite, none of whom any of us recognized. I assumed they were all part of Jay Killa's entourage. But the hip-hop star himself was notably absent. Where he could have been was anyone's guess. Perhaps he was in the adjacent suite being entertained by strippers, I thought, amused.

"I'm going downstairs to see what's the holdup on the food," Marcus said.

"Why can't you just call down there to the front desk?" I asked.

Marcus shook his head. "If there's one thing Mama D. always taught me, it's that you always get a better response when you handle your business in person. Killa asked me to help handle things for him. Besides, I wanna show Tommy around the hotel."

Marcus and Tommy headed out of the room and trudged down the hall. In the meantime, someone else had taken the liberty of turning up the music. Ariel and I, tired and reeling from all the festivities, sought solace by retreating to the bedroom. She got up from sitting in the main room, and I quickly followed her. So far, the bedroom, with its giant king-sized bed, was the only space in the suite unoccupied by anyone else. We set our purses down on the dresser, then sat on the side of the bed and simply talked.

"So… it sounds like somebody's headed for an engagement," I turned and muttered to my friend.

Ariel took out her compact mirror and began applying bright red lipstick. "Yeah. Let's hope he's serious and not just blowing hot air," she responded.

"Well, he sounded serious. Plus he wasn't drunk when he said it. So—"

"Hold that thought, I left my drink in the other room. I'll be right back."

Ariel rose from the bed and went to get her drink. In the meantime, I went to the bathroom to freshen up. I set my purse on top of the marble countertop as I waved a hand through my hair. Looking in the mirror, I could clearly see where a lack of sleep had taken its toll. Suddenly my cell phone buzzed in my purse. It was Mama, I knew, calling to see if I was okay. I'd felt guilty about not calling her ever since we'd arrived in LA.

I thumbed my phone alive. "Hello? Yes, Mama. We're here, and we're having fun. It's nice to see other parts of the country. Yes, ma'am, we're staying out of trouble." My mother kept me on the phone for at least fifteen minutes. She wanted to know about LA, Hollywood, if we'd seen any celebrities. But most of all she wanted to know about the airplane that had brought us here. It was inconceivable to Mama, having just come from horses and wagons as being the only mode of transportation, to black folks sitting inside of a steel tube and being flown across the country at thirty thousand feet in the air. I'd be lying if I said I wasn't terrified myself just at the thought of it.

After ending the call, I put my cell phone back in my purse and walked out relieved. I was glad to know that my mother was doing okay, despite the fact that she was staying by herself in my South Side apartment. Chicago had been making national headlines lately, and apparently for all the wrong reasons.

I walked inside of the bedroom, and my eyes were immediately drawn to the bed. I gasped at the sight of what I saw. Ariel was lying on top of the bed on her back with her legs splayed, her panties pulled down, hanging around one of her ankles. I threw my purse down and rushed over to her body. Her eyes were almost completely shut. She looked utterly lifeless.

I bolted out of the room. "What happened to my friend? Does anyone know? She needs an ambulance!"

At first, everyone just looked at me; they stared like I was speaking a foreign language. Then a young woman set her drink down and pulled out her cell phone to dial 911. Immediately I went back to get my purse and grabbed my phone to call Marcus and Tommy. I stayed by the bed. I didn't want to leave my friend's side and prayed that she was still alive. I looked around the room, and then noticed Ariel's almost-empty glass on the night-stand. Within several minutes I heard some commo-tion and knew that Tommy and Marcus had made it back into the suite. They both rushed inside the bedroom. Tommy was so upset he looked disoriented.

"Is an ambulance coming?" Tommy asked.

"They're on their way," I said nervously.

Tommy knelt over Ariel as she lay on the bed. "Hold on, baby, please. Help is on the way. I'm so sorry I left you," he said softly as he kissed her forehead.

After several minutes Marcus and Tommy went to the doorway, where onlookers had gathered. They both began asking everyone what happened. None of us knew what to think. *Did she simply pass out from drinking too much?* But that wouldn't explain how her panties had gotten around her ankles. *Had she been drugged? Or worse yet, raped?*

Marcus squared up to a group of men standing

near the bathroom. "What happened to my friend's girl in there? Somebody knows something. She's in there passed out with her panties around her ankles." Marcus looked around and sharply questioned what were at least fifteen people in the room now. I had never seen him this upset. He was ready to fight. A Hispanic girl in a tightfitting red dress moved away to turn off the stereo.

A squat guy wearing a black leather jacket was the first to actually respond. "I didn't see anything, man. There have been people coming in and out all night. Does Killa know about this yet?" he asked, shaking his head.

"No, Killa doesn't know anything. He hasn't even *been* here. Not in this suite." Marcus folded his arms and glared at the face of each partygoer. "So don't nobody know nothing? Not a damned thing?" he said in disbelief. Everyone in the room shook their heads. They stared blankly at each other.

The three of us were still searching for answers. And I wondered how long it would be before the ambulance arrived. Every minute counted. It would clearly be the difference between Ariel making it to the nearest hospital, or … death. That, I didn't even want to think about. I'd already spent more time in hospitals than I'd wanted to during my brief time in

Chicago. We quickly went back in the bedroom. Marcus walked around the bed and lifted up Ariel's wrist. I remembered him knowing how to check for vitals in case his grandmother ever went into complications from diabetes.

Marcus looked up at Tommy and me. "I can feel a slight pulse," he said.

"Shouldn't we call her parents?" I called out.

Tommy immediately went into panic mode. "No. Not yet. I don't want them tripping on her being out here until—"

"Until what? She's dead?" I spat furiously. "They're her parents, Tommy. They need to know!"

Suddenly I heard the mechanical clicks of a steel gurney being rolled over the carpet and into the suite. I turned around and saw two EMTs in white shirts and several LAPD officers enter the room. Marcus pulled out his cell phone and sent a text asking if someone could go next door to see if Jay Killa was there and if he was aware of what was happening.

"Did she drink or eat something?" one of the paramedics asked.

"Yeah. She had some champagne," I said, pointing to the glass on the nightstand.

The paramedics slipped on blue gloves and

began checking for Ariel's vital signs. The police asked the rest of us to step outside of the bedroom to give an account of everything that had happened leading up to this moment. I told them everything I knew. Everything that led up to me discovering Ariel lying on that bed.

One of the cops began interviewing everyone else in the suite. The other cop stood by the doorway and continued with Marcus, Tommy, and me. They asked who had rented the room. They had also asked where Ariel's parents were. Suddenly I turned toward the bedroom and saw the paramedics lifting Ariel to put her on the gurney. I watched as they rolled her past, still seemingly unconscious. Roughly forty minutes later, the police were finished with us. Then we called an Uber to take us to the hospital.

When we arrived in the emergency room at MetroWest, Tommy sought out the nearest nurse to give us an update. Marcus and I followed right behind him. Before we could get to the nurses' station, I watched Tommy bury his face in his hands. Marcus and I feared the worst. Tommy looked up. He looked crestfallen.

"They believe she was drugged and possibly fondled," he said, his voice cracking. "They've run some tests and found that date rape drug in her system."

Marcus shook his head, then rested his hand on Tommy's shoulder. "I'm sorry, man. I feel entirely responsible. I should have let you stay in the room with her."

Tommy shrugged in disgust. "Hey, it's not your fault, bro. Don't beat yourself up over it. You didn't know this kind of thing would happen."

I was devastated. Feelings of guilt swept through my body for leaving Ariel alone for the length of time that I did. "Where is she, and when can we see her?" I frantically asked the nurse who had given us the terrible news.

She was an older woman, heavyset, who looked like she'd hardened, maybe even lost some compassion after so many years of being on the job. The nurse looked up from behind her desk, where she was filling out a chart.

"You'll be able to see her … hopefully soon. The police are waiting until she's coherent so that they can speak with her. After that, I think that you can visit her. Two at a time."

Marcus's eyes locked on mine. "Had you not returned to that room when you did, things could have been a lot worse. I'm just thankful she's gonna be all right. We'll get through this, y'all."

I still struggled with the thought of calling Ariel's parents and telling them what had happened. I knew it was the right thing to do. I also knew that sometimes in life we don't always do what we think we should because of the effect it will have on others. I knew that her parents would go into an instant nuclear meltdown. I imagined that they would be on the next flight out of Chicago landing at LAX.

Marcus tapped me on the arm and nodded in the direction of several LAPD officers sauntering down the hall. Two uniformed cops and two people in plainclothes, one female. I assumed they were detectives. They walked past us, within arm's reach, and not surprisingly, they didn't notice that we were the same people they had interviewed at the hotel.

The fact that they went into one of the rooms led me to believe that Ariel was now awake and coherent. I looked at Marcus and Tommy and then motioned them to start walking. The three of us eased our way closer to the room. We looked around at opposite ends of the hall and pretended to be lost. Standing in front of a hand sanitizer dispenser attached to the wall, I could vaguely hear the police as they questioned Ariel. I pressed the lever at the bottom of the dispenser and a rope of white foam fell into my hand.

Ariel still sounded somewhat groggy when she talked. Suddenly, there was some commotion in the room. "Hurry, grab that bag on the floor!" one of the cops yelled.

The three of us moved toward the entrance of the room and looked inside. Ariel was leaning over the bed. Holding her stomach, she heaved violently into a paper bag the police had propped in front of her. I looked at Tommy as he shook his head. He started to go inside.

"No, Tommy. Wait!" I whispered.

A few moments later a male nurse wearing light blue scrubs came toward us carrying some towels and cleaning items. We moved so that he could enter the room. The police continued talking and jotting notes while the nurse made sure that Ariel's gown, bed, and the floor were clean. I saw Ariel briefly look past the officer who had been doing most of the talking. Her eyes darted away as she met my gaze squarely and smiled.

About twenty minutes later, one of the plainclothes officers reached into his pocket and left his card on the dinner tray next to Ariel's bed. The three of us walked down the hall in an effort not to be noticed. As soon as the police ventured out of the room, we trudged back and went inside.

Ariel brightened when she saw us come in. Tommy leaned over and hugged and kissed her. Marcus and I immediately did the same. Ariel pushed a button and made the bed more elevated.

"How are you feeling?" Tommy asked.

"Better, but still nauseous."

"So, what did the police say? They have any leads yet?" Tommy asked as he grabbed a chair from the corner and moved it closer to the bed. Marcus and I found two more chairs and moved them to the other side and sat.

"They told me that there were no witnesses. But they have the glass of champagne that I drank from and are testing it for fingerprints other than mine. The doctor said that I tested positive for Rohypnol." Ariel ran a hand through her hair. "Fortunately, whatever the jerk who did this had in mind, he didn't get to finish the job."

Tommy lowered his head and exhaled deeply. The first thing I thought was how could this trip to LA start out so adventurous and fun, then end up on such a sour note. I was just thankful that things weren't as bad as they could have been. And also grateful that my best friend was going to be all right.

Marcus leaned forward and held out his hands in front of him. "Ariel, I just want to say how truly sorry I am that this has happened to you. If I hadn't taken Tommy out of the room, I'm sure that this would not have occurred. But rest assured, I'm going to do all I can to find out who did it."

"Marcus, stop feeling guilty. It's not your fault; life happens. What about my parents? Do they know? Did either of you tell them?" Ariel asked nervously, looking around.

I answered. "No. But they really need to—"

"What, Lula? Find out so they can lecture me for the next two months? My mom's blood pressure is already off the rails, and I'll never get to live it down. Especially, like, with alcohol being involved? My dad would absolutely lose his mind." Ariel tossed her hair back. "It was a good lesson learned. I should have never left my drink unattended." Then she reached for the remote to power on the room's television. "Anyhow, the doctor said that in a few days, I should be discharged. And I have also been contacted by several attorneys."

"What about the rest of the police investiga-tion? How is that going to work if they need to follow up with you, or meet with you in person?" I said.

"They have my cell number, and I gave them Tommy's address as my mailing address. If I need to appear in person for any reason, I'll just come back to LA if necessary. At this point, I just want to go home."

We stayed by Ariel's bedside for most of the night and up until dawn. After the effects of the drug wore off, she seemed to be her usual self again. She was alert and full of bustling energy. Even her sense of humor had become evident. As we left the hospital to go back to our hotel, Marcus called United Airlines' customer service to reschedule our flight back to Chicago. At this point, we didn't care about any additional fees or costs we might have to pay. We were simply looking forward to going home, back to our lives.

We summoned a cab and arrived at our hotel, an inexpensive place we'd found on West Olympic Boulevard. During the next twenty-four hours, we remained low-key, not venturing out except to pick up breakfast, and then some Chinese takeout for dinner. I could tell by Marcus's demeanor that something about this LA experience had humbled him.

While he'd been on his cell phone for roughly fifteen minutes checking on Mama D., Ariel had sent a text that she was being discharged as of 9:30 this morning. The timing could not have been more perfect, because our flight was scheduled to leave for Chicago at 1 p.m. When he disconnected the call, he came over to my side of the room, pulled me into his embrace, and gently kissed my forehead.

"It's always nice to get away, to visit other places. But after a while you definitely begin to miss home," he said.

"I agree." My eyes locked onto his. "Like you, I'm ready to go."

CHAPTER 11

TWO DAYS later I arrived at work early for a meeting with Gladys Brennan, the school's superintendent. After finishing my usual morning cup of green tea, I ventured into a conference room where eleven of my colleagues were already seated. I had absolutely no idea what this meeting was about.

But what I *did* know was that it was mandatory for the entire teaching staff at L. Bowers Elementary to attend. The first bombshell that had been dropped on me was that Mrs. Connie Jacoby, the teacher who I was hired to assist, had just requested five days of sick leave. On top of that, the pool of substitute teachers was so low, and other teachers in the school so overburdened, that by the time capable help was found, Mrs. Jacoby would be back in class. So I was now being formally notified that I would take over her class in her absence.

The meeting lasted for about an hour. But the fact that Mrs. Jacoby would be missing in action for a few days was not the main topic of discussion. What it boiled down to was the powers that be wanted to let everyone know of the school's bleak future. Its very likelihood of remaining open hinged on how well the kids progressed by the end of the academic year. Most of us teachers and staff were devastated. Not only for the sake of the children, who had already been the victims of one too many district closings and had to be consolidated into existing, already overcrowded schools, but also for us as educators, whose primary area of expertise was in special education. How likely would it be that we could readily find new employment?

I left the conference room stressed, then filed into my classroom, which was filled with energetic and hyperactive kids. Still, I remained positive throughout the day, even when it came time to face parents at the end of my last class. As I stood behind my desk at 2:47 p.m., putting away extra supplies, crayons, and pencils, my eyes were immediately drawn to the center of the room. One of the students was still sitting in his chair, with his head buried in his arms.

His name was Malcolm Warner. He was your typical student, with a special talent that I'd noted in the past—the ability to draw really well. Concerned, I walked over to his desk.

"Malcolm, why are you still here? Are you all right?"

He raised his head slowly and shook it from side to side. I could tell he'd been crying.

"I want to kill myself," he said.

I stood there, shocked. "Why would you say something like that? What's bothering you?" I asked him. "And what are you drawing?" I picked up a white sheet of paper from his desk and saw that Malcolm had drawn a sketch of a person hanging by what looked like a noose.

"They bully me. They talk about the way I look and about us being so poor. So I don't want to live any longer, Ms. Darling. I just want to die."

I could not believe that this boy of only eight years old had gotten so depressed that he wanted to actually end his life. I grabbed one of the desks nearby and pulled it over to sit next to him. "Look at me," I said, facing him sternly. "You have to be strong, Malcolm. You have to love yourself enough

to not ever let someone else's opinion of you matter.
Their words cannot physically harm you. Because if
you give up, guess what? The bullies win. And I
don't want that. I want *you* to win. You're a winner
whether you know it or not, Malcolm. Believe it or
not, *I* was bullied in school. But I just brushed it off
and kept going. And you know what? Things got
better from that point on. The one mistake I made,
and the one you and so many other kids make, is
that they don't tell anyone. Anyone that's being
bullied should tell their parents, their teachers,
someone in a position of authority who can put a
stop to it. We all deserve a chance at living a long
and happy life. And what someone else says about
you, or me, should not change any of that."

I folded the piece of paper of Malcolm's drawing, walked to the front of the room and put it
inside my purse. Then I walked back to his desk.
"What would your mother have to say about this?
And where is she now?"

Malcolm glanced up and met my gaze, thank-
fully maintaining steady eye contact. "I don't know
what she'd say. I don't think she would care. She's at
home … I think."

"Come on. I'm taking you home. I'm going to
need to speak with your mother." The two of us left

the classroom and walked out to my car. As we made the ten-minute trek through the community of Washington Park, I was pleased to see that Malcolm at least knew how to tell someone where he lived.

We pulled in front of a greystone duplex. I got out of my car and opened the passenger door for Malcolm. We went inside the foyer of the building, and Malcolm immediately pushed the buzzer for his mother to let us in through a second door. Once the door buzzed, he led me down a short flight of stairs to what appeared to be a garden apartment below ground.

A woman who looked to be in her late forties opened the door. Hanging from her mouth was an unlit cigarette. She was wearing a tightfitting pair of faded jeans and a T-shirt that said: What you NOT gone do is...

Immediately I extended my hand as Malcolm ran past his mother to go inside. "Ms. Warner, I'm Lula Darling. I'm filling in for Malcolm's teacher."

"What? He in some kind of trouble or something?"

"No, no, not really. But I need to talk to you about your son if I may."

"All right. Come in."

I looked briefly around the apartment. The condition of it was borderline deplorable. There were plates of leftover food on the floor. Piles of clothes and cardboard boxes saturated the living room. And dashing across the carpeted floor was a beige-and-white kitten that had seemingly chased something under the sofa. Malcolm's mother grabbed several bulging dark green garbage bags from off the couch and tossed them into a corner.

"Have a seat," she said and tilted her head. "Now I wanna hear what you felt was so important that you had to come to my house to tell me."

I sat on the sofa, holding my purse in my lap. "The reason I'm here, Ms. Warner, is because Malcolm said that he's being bullied at school."

Ms. Warner burst out laughing. She leaned backward, holding her stomach as if I'd just delivered the greatest punchline she'd ever heard.

"Is that it? He's being bullied? Well, why don't we call 911? Or better yet, why don't we call the mayor's office? As if there ain't more serious things going on in this hellhole of a city. Hell, I was bullied when I was a kid. We all were bullied at one point or another. As long as they don't put they hands on my child, to me—it ain't that big of a deal."

"But it *is* a big deal. Kids are committing suicide

nationwide because of bullying. Just because you or I may have been able to brush it off doesn't mean that Malcolm is capable of doing the same."

Ms. Warner shook her head. Then she lit her cigarette and proceeded to blow a cloud of smoke toward the ceiling. "I'll tell you what the problem is. You want me to tell you what the problem is with these kids today?"

I nodded. "Please."

"The problem with these kids today is that they weak. Yeah, that's right, I said it. When I was comin' up, we didn't get everything we wanted. And when we got outta line, our parents put a belt to our backside. Nowadays, these kids wanna call the police when you whip their butts. Or if they can't get what they want, they wanna rob or kill for it! So what's the answer, you might ask? Here it is ... we need to stop this madness of being their friend instead of being a parent and get in these kids' behinds."

I looked at Ms. Warner as she sat on a clothes-filled plastic container across the room. I imagined that her rage and frustration came deep from within, stemming from the realization that the same system that enabled others to achieve the American dream often made it more difficult for people that looked like her and me. I wondered if she applied her beliefs about raising a child to her own son.

"Malcolm is different," I told her. "He's a good kid with a special talent. He's a really good artist, in case you haven't noticed. However, today, in my classroom, he said that he wanted to kill himself." I opened my purse and pulled out the folded piece of paper with Malcolm's sketch. "He drew this picture of a person hanging. This is a serious matter, Ms. Warner. I believe this is the way he wanted to kill himself."

"Let me see that."

I handed the sketch to Ms. Warner.

"Sometimes these kids … they just want attention. I don't think he had it in him to do this. I really don't." After studying the drawing for several seconds, she glanced up at me. "They labeled Malcolm as being educable retarded. That is the only reason he in your school."

"A lot of kids are given that label unmistakably. Your son just needs that extra push to get up to speed. I believe he has a bright future ahead of him if given the proper support."

Ms. Warner stared at the paper, eyeing it with what seemed like a more serious demeanor. My hope was that I had gotten through to her. The last thing I wanted to do was to notify Child Protective Services. I wanted to give Malcolm and his mother the opportunity to get everything right before I sought any outside assistance.

"I'm going to report the kids involved to the administration. I'm sure disciplinary action will be taken," I said.

Ms. Warner looked up, her expression still somewhat defiant. It was almost as if she didn't want to give me any credit for anything I had said during my visit. "I will talk to my son. Thank you for bringing him home."

"You're more than welcome," I said as I turned to leave the apartment. I purposely left the sketch that Malcolm had drawn as a reminder that her son needed an immediate intervention. Then I got in my car to drive home. On the way there, I hoped I'd made a difference in the life of little Malcolm Warner, and that someday, he would go on to do great things.

CHAPTER 12

I WAS busy grading papers after school, pressed between finishing and watching the early evening news, when there was a heavy knock on the door. I set down my marker and the stack of diagnostic tests, smoothed the wrinkles from my blouse and headed toward the doorway. "Yes? Who is it?"

"It's Pastor Tompkins from First Deliverance. If this isn't a good time, I can certainly come back another day."

Curious, I opened the door. Pastor Tompkins stood in the hallway in his usual pressed pinstriped suit and polished black shoes. He smiled with an even set of extremely bright teeth. I was surprised that he had paid us an unexpected visit. The first thing I wondered was if something was wrong. My expression must have given me away.

"Please, don't be alarmed, Lula. I was in the neighborhood dropping off some things at the church and wanted to stop by and talk to you and your mother. May I come in?"

"Sure. My mother is in the room watching television. And I was just finishing up some papers for my students. I'll get her, and we can sit in the living room."

"That would be nice," he murmured.

"Can I get you anything, coffee or tea?" I asked.

"Oh, no, thank you. I just had lunch at the restaurant down the street with a few of the church's deacons. That should hold me for quite a while."

I went to get Mama from her bedroom. She had dozed off while watching an old rerun of *Grey's Anatomy*, which was her favorite pastime whenever she wasn't trying to learn a new skill, like how to operate a device or even a computer. After a slowdown at the restaurant where she worked, my mother had been given three days off with the promise that she'd be called back whenever business picked up.

Mama came into the living room, and Pastor Tompkins rose from the sofa to give her a big hug.

"Ella Mae, so good to see you, my dear sister," he said, beaming.

"How are things at the church?" Mama asked.

"Quite well, thank you for asking. Our member-ship has grown quite a bit over the last decade. But we still have some work to do to get more young people involved. I hope to see you and Lula there with Delores Whitaker more often."

"I like your church. Everyone made us feel at home, and I expect to join very soon."

Pastor Tompkins nodded as he sat on the couch. "That would be great. We'd be glad to have both you and Lula join, whenever you ladies are ready," he said as he clasped his hands in his lap. "But the reason I'm here today is because—well, let me be the first to say that I applaud you for your coura-geous efforts in trying to turn things around for our people, Lula."

"Thank you, Pastor. There is a lot that needs to be done. These are some serious times for black people, serious times for all people," I replied.

"I couldn't agree with you more. And as I'm sure you are aware, these are some troubling and turbulent times in which we live. My concern is that a young lady like yourself will be up against a formidable adversary. Against resistance from the lowest levels of wickedness all the way to the top. May I ask … what type of plan do you have to see this through?"

"I don't want to reveal everything I have in mind at this point. But I realize I can't do this alone. Along with God's help and the efforts of many—I want to start a new revolution."

Pastor Tompkins looked quite surprised by this. I'm sure he hadn't expected those types of words to spill forth from my mouth. And at the expense of sounding arrogant, I imagined that because of his age, he came from an entirely different era. I honestly felt that anyone who sought change today was going to have to approach things in a very different manner.

"I'm not trying to scare you. But allow me to show you something." The pastor reached into his suit jacket and pulled out a small manila envelope. "These are some newspaper clippings that I've saved, during just the last three years, mind you." On top of the glass table in the living room, Pastor Tompkins unfolded four articles. "Each of these people, three men and one woman, were community activists on the South Side. They were trying to do what *you* are doing; my guess is on a much smaller scale. Each one of them was working to combat gangs, drugs, and violence in their neighborhood. Each one ended up being shot on the street near their place of work or near their residence."

I pulled each article toward me and looked at the black-and-white photos of the deceased. I read the first paragraph of each and was reminded of the danger that I was putting myself in—especially after talking to Boogie at the town hall meeting.

Pastor Tompkins drew in a deep breath. He looked at me and then at Mama. "If I can be completely honest with both of you ... I think you should leave this kind of effort to someone else."

Someone else? Did he really just say that? "This is something I feel in my heart to do," I corrected. "I truly feel like God brought us here for a much bigger purpose. Although it was all around us in 1852, I did not fear death then, and I certainly don't fear it now. Just like the slaves that prayed and sang along with us in our quarters, who died so that black people could have the opportunities and freedom they now have, I don't mind dying today if it means that my people and future generations will be better off tomorrow."

Pastor Tompkins leaned forward and slowly extended his hand. "All I wanted to do is come here and speak to you from the heart, my dear sister. Please know that the church is always available to help, however we can. I'll be praying for you both."

CHAPTER 13

THE FOLLOWING MORNING, Gladys Brennan, the embattled superintendent who ran L. Bowers Elementary with an ironclad fist, summoned me to her office once again. She'd promised our little session would take no longer than fifteen minutes max, so I arrived thirty minutes early just to be sure that I was in class on time.

When I entered her office, she was sitting behind her desk, talking on the phone and peering out the window at a construction project going on behind the school. A few seconds later, she smoothly spun her chair around and jerked her chin forward to acknowledge my presence.

"Good morning, Lula. I was talking to a procurement specialist about why we can't seem to get any new furniture for our students. But I think I already know the answer." Gladys got up from behind her desk and closed the door to her office.

"I wanted to have you come in this morning to talk to you about one of your kids."

"Which one?"

"Malcolm Warner. You paid him and his mom a visit at their home the other day?"

I nodded. "Yes. He was the last one in class. He told me that he'd been bullied, so I gave him a ride home and then talked to his mother about what had happened. I also reported it to Assistant Principal Kelly the following day. Why, did I do something wrong?"

Gladys leaned back against her office chair, clasped her hands in front of her and hiked one leg over the other. "School guidelines require that permission is obtained from both the parent and my office to give a student a ride home. But even so, that's not the real issue here. Malcolm's mother has informed us that she'll be keeping him out of school for a while. She's also seeking legal counsel and contemplating bringing charges against the school."

My boss's words cut through me sharp. I slowly shook my head in disbelief. "I don't understand. When I visited her in her home, she seemed to think it wasn't that big of a deal. She scoffed at the whole idea of a child being bullied as long as the child was not physically harmed. She even thanked me before I left."

"Sometimes people have time to think. Sometimes they talk to someone else, or perhaps they see something on the news that gets them to act a certain way. The bottom line is, with the threat of our school closing, we can't afford to have declining attendance. I know you're merely filling in temporarily for Connie. I just wanted to give you a heads-up. As things develop and we get a better sense of what Ms. Warner's true intentions are, I'll be sure to keep you abreast of the situation."

I couldn't believe how bad my day had gotten before it even got started. "Thank you. Please do," I said. Then I rose from the chair in front of Gladys's desk and turned to leave her office.

After school was over, I felt an urgent need to a break away from anything that even remotely seemed like work. With the heavy burden of my job taking its toll, along with attending night classes at DePaul, getting the Movement off the ground, I'd started to feel like I was coming apart at the seams. Immediately I called my friends, including Marcus, to see if they were available to meet for either an early dinner or a late-afternoon lunch.

As it turned out, Marcus had to be downtown at 6 p.m. to meet with an entertainment attorney about his contract. That left us with about three hours to find a bite to eat. Ariel had been working part-time and going to school three nights a week, so she was available too. Tommy couldn't make it. Fortunately, he had found a job despite having a few blemishes on his record and couldn't get off work until almost 10 p.m.

The three of us agreed on a casual restaurant in the heart of downtown Chicago. I was the first to arrive, followed by Marcus, and then Ariel. It would be some much-needed me time after the stressful day I'd had, and considering everything else I wanted to accomplish going forward—my life's purpose.

"You know, I heard the burgers are really good here. That's what one of my mom's friends said. Of course, everyone's taste buds are different," Ariel said.

Marcus shook his head while looking at the menu. "I don't care. I'm so hungry I could eat just about anything right now. Do y'all know those fools kept me in the studio all day, going over and over the same part of the song! They kept arguing with each other about which version of the chorus was better."

"Who? What are you talking about?" I asked while crunching on tortilla chips and salsa.

"They're this new group I'm producing. One of them sings, one of them raps, and the other dude plays all the instruments. They call themselves 'trying to do something different.' Actually, you almost *have* to if you want to stand out in today's market. So I gotta give them their props for that."

A waitress came over to take our order. The three of us ordered grass-fed beef burgers with fries and hand-spun milkshakes. Both my diet and my appetite were so much different now compared to what they'd been in the past. Usually, after work, I would eat a good home-cooked meal around 6 p.m. at the dinner table with Mama. But today … I was going to allow myself to completely pig out.

"I've been in contact with an attorney who's out in L.A.," Ariel announced. "He wants to bring charges against the hotel for negligence and for not providing adequate security due to a lack of working security cameras in the common areas."

"So what are you thinking? What are you going to do?" I asked.

"I'm not sure. I've been talking it over with

Tommy. I'm afraid that somehow my parents are going to find out. Then they'll be even more pissed that I didn't tell them from the start."

"What about any information on who it was that assaulted you? Do the police have—at least a person of interest?" Marcus asked.

"Um, no. Not to my knowledge. If they haven't arrested anyone by now, I don't think they ever will. If they're even trying, for that matter."

Marcus bit into his burger. "I asked Killa's people out in LA if they knew anything, and of course nobody knows nothing. And you being a white girl? I figured they'd have at least *three* brothers in custody by now."

I glared at Marcus for the off-color comment.

"What? I'm just saying … it's the truth," he said.

Ariel chuckled.

"Why are you laughing?" I asked her, smiling.

She took a sip from her shake. "I just remembered the look on your face in the limo, when you had no idea who O.J. was."

"Well, it's not like I didn't have a good excuse. I'll be the first to admit that I have a lot of catching up to do."

Ariel dipped a French fry into a small plastic

cup of ketchup. "It won't be hard for you to learn what happened during *that* trial. Both the media *and* the public were thrown into a friggin' frenzy."

"Speaking of which." Marcus nodded his head forward, signaling for Ariel and me to turn around in our seats. For several minutes he'd been completely silent. Ariel and I had our backs turned toward Michigan Avenue, and I had wondered what he could have been staring at while looking out the window.

I turned around and saw a group of people slowly begin to swell in the middle of the street. I got up from the table and walked closer to the glass to see for myself what exactly was happening. "Whatever it is that's about to go down doesn't quite look good," I said.

It was rush hour. An overcast day with strong winds and a slight drizzle steadily coming in off the lake. Cars and buses had stopped, not wanting to run over the group of protesters. I counted at least thirty, with linked arms, creating a human roadblock as they stood in solidarity. A middle-aged black man suddenly raised a white bullhorn he'd been holding in his right hand.

He shouted, "Sixteen shots and a cover-up!" Then boomed repeatedly, "Hands up. Don't shoot!"

The rest of the crowd joined in the chant as they stood in the rain.

Marcus and Ariel got up from their seats and joined me at the window. "They're talking about police shootings, white supremacy, and the case where that video was released of the cop that shot that young brother sixteen times," Marcus said.

As each passing minute went by, we watched the crowd grow larger. More police had arrived to compensate for the growing numbers of people. Some of the police officers sat on bicycles wearing black helmets and rain gear. Some were even mounted on horses. It was clear that the demonstrators intended on making a statement by shutting down Michigan Avenue. If so, they'd picked the perfect place to do it. I remembered similar protests last year on Black Friday, the busiest shopping day of the year.

As I looked out the rain-splattered window, I saw that it wasn't only black people marching outside. There were whites and Latinos, too. As a news crew partially blocked our view, and as people came together for justice and a common cause, at this moment, I thought there were no differences in education, socioeconomic background, or skin color, just people of the human family, collectively standing up for what was right.

I didn't know all the details about this case. And I'd never been involved in a live protest before. But I knew that a seventeen-year-old young man had been brutally murdered. I also knew that something did not sit right in my conscience, and I felt compelled to join the march. By now, the crowd looked to be in the hundreds if not thousands. I looked at both Marcus and Ariel. Since it had been my invitation for lunch, I insisted on covering our meal, even against Marcus's offer to pay. "Today is on me. I'd like to go outside."

The three of us grabbed our belongings and made our way onto the sidewalk. Horns were blowing relentlessly. Traffic had been stagnated for as far down as I could see. It was beginning to look like a standoff between protesters and the police. Several officers watched us as we moved toward the curb. Immediately I saw several large handwritten signs in the midst of the sea of people: "NO JUSTICE, NO PEACE!" "NO MORE KKKiller Cops!" There were different ages among the faces in the crowd. Many were holding umbrellas.

The three of us merged into the middle of the group, between what looked like a throng of college students and an older white man wearing gold-rimmed glasses. As we became part of the cause, I imagined that this was also personal for Marcus, whose younger brother, Fred, had somehow been killed while in police custody. I looked at my best friend and my boyfriend, and together we raised our fists in solidarity and cycled through chants, repeating the slogans of someone near the front of the crowd. With one hand, I retrieved my cell phone from my purse and began recording. Facing us on our left were policemen on their bikes near the curb. Suddenly there was pushing and shoving, and someone cursed. The police began to shift and move as if they were ready to start making arrests. I wondered if they had just gotten a directive to either control or disperse the crowd.

Someone behind us pushed us forward into an approaching wall of cops. Two of the policemen lurched forward and then wrestled Marcus onto the ground. "We weren't doing anything but marching. We were pushed!" I cried.

One of the cops pointed his baton at us. "Shut up now, or you're going to jail!"

"You have no right to arrest any of us!" Ariel yelled as she was being restrained.

"For civil disobedience," one of the officers shouted back.

The police pinned Marcus facedown on the ground and zipped a plastic tie around his wrists behind his back. I saw him straining, trying desperately to keep me in his line of sight, the muscles in his neck bulging in panic. Then Marcus was hauled off to a waiting police van near the intersection of Michigan Avenue and Adams Street.

"Let's follow them in my car, Ariel." Ariel had been released from a nearby cop's grip, and she followed me to a parking garage around the corner. I figured that they were taking Marcus to the 1st District Police Station on South State Street. It was a building I was already intimately familiar with from the night I'd turned myself in to government authorities, a night when, to my surprise, and as a silver lining, I had been reunited with Mama.

When we arrived at the station, there were already several police vans with detained demonstrators parked in the middle of the street. Several officers who had apparently been driving, accompanied by several more who had exited the station, slowly opened the doors so that the protesters could be taken into the building. I knew that Marcus had to be in one of the two vans. I turned toward Ariel. "You think we should call Mama D.? I'm not trying to make her any more sick than she already is."

Ariel nodded. "I would if I were you, Lula. This is serious. And it's the right thing to do. Besides, who else has the money to bail him out?"

I pulled out my cell phone and reluctantly called Marcus's grandmother. Ironically, when I reached her, she had been cooking and watching the protests unfold on local news media. I knew that my call would send her into panic mode and that she was going to have to find a way to come downtown immediately.

After ending the call, Ariel and I waited for the protesters to file into the station. Then we got out of my car and walked through the revolving glass door to go inside. There was already a line of people in front of us talking to officers about someone they knew who had been brought in.

For a brief moment, I considered asking Ariel to tell her parents what had happened. I wondered if they *did* make the trip to the South Loop, if they would have considered paying for Marcus's bail. Not so much for him, because they barely knew him, but for me, considering that he was my boyfriend. Between whatever cash Marcus and I had on hand, we would have certainly paid them back and then some.

I prayed to God that when Mama D. arrived, she would have the means to post the required bail to get Marcus released. I also prayed to God that Marcus would not be slapped with any trumped-up charges, that he would be granted bail and actually sleep in his own bed tonight. Anyone with raw footage of the protests would be able to clearly see that he did not, in any way, shape, or form, attack that cop.

A burly policeman came walking near a group of us who had been waiting. He announced that we'd need to stand out of the way and keep the corridor open for additional foot traffic coming in off State Street. He explained that if we were waiting for someone being detained, that we might as well prepare to be holed up for a long, disappointing night. And that most of the protesters would have their belongings confiscated and be taken to a holding area. The police officer walked back to where he'd been seated, and among the banter with other cops, I heard someone mention *Black Lives Matter*, just as a young black man was brought through the entrance in steel handcuffs.

As Ariel and I waited for Mama D. to arrive, a

black woman standing next to us started talking. "It doesn't make any sense how many times they shot that boy. My son, even at the tender age of nineteen knew there needed to be a protest. That's why I'm here. They arrested my boy." She pulled out her cell phone, thumbed it alive and began showing Ariel and me pictures of her son on prom and on the night he'd graduated.

He was a clean-cut and handsome young man. "You must be very proud of him. Especially with what the dropout rate is among students here in the city," I said.

"I am. I'm very proud of him. We don't live in the greatest of neighborhoods. And his older brother, God rest his soul, was shot and killed last summer in a case of mistaken identity."

"We're so sorry for your loss," Ariel and I told her.

"Thank you. That's why I stay on my youngest son so much. I can't afford to lose two to this sense-less violence. But Tariq," she said, shaking her head, "he sure knows he loves to run these streets. Although, fortunately, most of his friends that he's been close to over the years have now moved to the suburbs, so he spends most of his time out there."

On her face, I could see the pain that death had

still managed to inflict. And I was hoping, like I had hoped for Marcus, that this woman's son would not be railroaded into being criminally charged. Not everyone, of course, could afford to have a lawyer present while in custody, even though I'd heard of some relatively inexpensive prepaid legal service plans that would have been a godsend at a time like this. I wished it were something that Marcus had gotten for himself.

"Despite being arrested tonight, I know that Tariq bears no ill will toward these police officers." She smiled, almost as if embarrassed. "You want to hear something funny and ironic?"

"Sure."

"Well, Tariq says that once he graduates from college, he wants to be one of them. He wants to be a Chicago police officer."

Ariel and I chuckled. "That *is* very ironic. And it's also quite impressive that at such a young age, he knows exactly what he wants to do with his life."

The woman, whose name we still did not know, drew in a deep breath. "I think that after what happened to his brother, he wants to somehow make a difference. He wants to offer a familiar face in the community he serves. Hopefully what happened tonight won't affect his chances."

I turned to my right at the sound of some commotion. Coming through the revolving door was Mama D., along with Pastor Tompkins. "Lula, what's the latest?" she asked nervously. She hobbled toward Ariel and me, supported by her cane on her right side and the pastor's hand holding her left arm. Her eyes darted between me, Ariel, and the cops that were in the area.

I walked in her direction and gave her a hug. "They have him in a holding area," I said, pointing toward the back of the station. "I don't know what he's being charged with or when he'll be—"

"I'm here about my grandson, Marcus Whitaker. He's being detained, and I want to know why?" Mama D. turned to one of the officers sitting behind a desk and asked.

A young Hispanic cop stood up from his seat. "He might be here for anything, from … civil disobedience, to unlawful assembly, to assault of a police officer. Either way, you're looking at probably the morning before he can be released. And there are no visitations."

Marcus's grandmother shook her head. "He did not do *any* of those things that you're accusing him of. He was simply exercising his right to protest peacefully. Why is it you didn't arrest any of the white demonstrators?"

The officer shrugged. "How do you know what race they are?"

"I saw the arrests live on the evening news, and my grandson's girlfriend recorded her own footage with her cell phone." Mama D. became visibly upset and pointed. "I bet the majority of the people you have back there, wherever they are, are black, aren't they? This is exactly why there are problems between the police and the black community!"

Pastor Tompkins rested his hands on her shoulders in an attempt to calm her down. "Delores, we have to abide by what the officer has said," he murmured. "Now if we have to, we can come back first thing in the morning and do what we can. One of the church's members is a criminal defense attorney. Even though it's on really short notice, it doesn't hurt to ask him if he can assist us."

After twenty minutes of standing on her feet, Mama D. was ready for Pastor Tompkins to take her home. She vowed to be back here first thing in the morning whether flanked by an attorney or not. Ariel and I waited for forty-five more minutes before I took her back to her car, where we were met by the sight of more people being brought in for whatever crimes they were being accused of. Ariel's parents hadn't heard from her, and my mother had been calling me relentlessly every hour, wondering about my whereabouts and when I would be home.

At roughly eight the following morning, Ariel and I arrived at the police station within minutes of each other. Not long afterward, a third car pulled up, and I saw Pastor Tompkins slowly assist Mama D. onto the sidewalk. After greeting each other and jointly hoping for an easy resolution, the four of us trudged into the station together.

Mama D. was immediately referred to an officer who had been assigned to handle inquiries about arrests made during the protests. We must have looked odd being here the way we were, almost like a complete family unit, which was becoming increasingly rare, statistically speaking. I glanced over at Pastor Tompkins, and while he generally looked pleased to be with us this morning, he also looked as if he'd been suppressing his disdain for how far I was willing to commit to my cause.

Standing not far from us was another small

group of people desperately inquiring about the release of their family members. The officer instructed all of us to be patient while she looked into the status of who was expected to be released.

So you could imagine the looks on our faces when we saw Marcus walking toward us from the back of the building. Everyone beamed and collectively greeted him with a tight hug.

"Boy, you always seem to find yourself smack dab in the middle of something. Although at least this time, I can say it was for a noble cause," Mama D. called out.

Marcus glanced up and smiled at her. "So, I take it you're not mad at me?"

"Well, I'd be lying if I said I wasn't disappointed when I left here last night. But overnight I had time to think about it. And I realized that when it comes to things like civil rights and justice, nothing was ever accomplished without somebody taking a stand for what they felt was right."

Marcus exhaled deeply. "All I know is that I'm ready to go home. I need to find out how to get my cell phone back, and my wallet and keys. Not having my phone is why I couldn't call anybody."

I watched as Marcus went to talk to someone about retrieving his personal belongings. Slowly, it appeared that more people were being released into the company of their loved ones. There was a young couple wearing dreads, shaking their heads and mumbling expletives underneath their breath. There was an older man who appeared disoriented. He kept looking around and asking if anyone had seen his wife because she had his medicine he desperately needed to take. Then came a Caucasian man in plainclothes, a badge around his neck and a large metal gun holstered on his right side. He was clean-shaven with small bags beneath his eyes, and a head of dark hair streaked with silver. He was carrying a mug in his left hand.

He pointed a finger at me. "Are you the young lady that fights against crime?"

I held up my head and squarely met his gaze. "Yes, my name is Lula. Lula Darling."

"Detective Ryan Laurence," he said, extending his right hand. "I remembered you from the town hall meeting on the South Side not that long ago. I was working the crowd undercover that night. Whenever the mayor appears somewhere, of course there's going to be a heightened need for security. I understand you're planning on becoming more visible in your efforts to combat crime and violence in the city. Is that correct?"

I nodded, wanting to remain congenial. But I also wondered what had prompted this guy to approach me totally out of nowhere. "Yes, that's right. I know that you and the rest of the police department are doing the best job you can, but I feel that it couldn't hurt to have additional resources to help you in your efforts."

Detective Laurence put one hand into his pocket and took a sip from his mug. "I couldn't agree with you more. We certainly welcome any help we can get from the public, especially with the current climate of community and police relations being what it is. That being said … we've got contacts on the streets in almost every district. And the streets always talk. Maybe not to the police, mind you, because people are either scared, or they're abiding by that dumb no-snitching rule. But word has gotten around about you and other similar community activists. And most of you still reside in the neighborhoods you're trying to clean up. While it's a commendable thing on its own, therein lies the danger with what you're doing. You become a sitting target for the bad guys." The detective took another sip from his cup.

"I'm not going to take up a lot of your time this morning. I know you're anxious to get home with your family. Just watch yourself out here." He reached into his shirt pocket. "Here's my card with all of my contact info. If you ever need me, don't hesitate to call me. Not all cops are bad cops."

I took the detective's card and inserted it into my purse. "Thank you for the words of caution."

He turned to walk away. Marcus returned shortly after he'd gotten his belongings, and the five of us left the police station and stepped out into the early-morning light bathing South State Street. Although severe weather had been forecast for later, right now it was clear, it was hot, and the warmth of the sun felt good on my skin.

Pastor Tompkins saw this as an opportunity to seize the moment. "Before we go on our separate paths this morning, I feel it is only right and proper that we give God His due. Things did not have to go as well as they did during the preceding twenty-four hours. Let us hold hands and bow our heads in prayer, for not only was Marcus unharmed during yesterday's emotional protests, but he has also not been charged with any crime."

CHAPTER 14

THE END of each day during summer school at L. Bowers Elementary was one of my proudest moments as an educator, not only because there were kids that needed extra class time to learn, but because school could give them a safe haven instead of being on the streets, potentially becoming the next victim of senseless violence. I watched patiently as the kids from my class charged out of the room. Anxiously, they bolted from the building to climb into one of the many yellow buses parked outside. The rest climbed into their parents' cars. Not a care in the world. Little did they know how good they had it, especially if they'd been able to compare their childhood with mine.

That conversation would have to be for another time. The weekend was approaching, and for the next several days there would be no school. I gathered papers and teaching materials from the top of my desk and began my own trek home.

No more stress. No more threats of being sued. No more worrying about whether I would have a job come next week.

As I got in my car and started the engine, my cell phone buzzed inside my purse's lined pocket. I swiped the screen and saw that it was a text, an invitation from Marcus inviting Mama and me to his house for a Fourth of July cookout.

Instantly, I replied back: *Yes, please, count us in.* The invite was a surprise, yet refreshing. Marcus had never mentioned to me, not once, that Mama D. ever liked to have company on any of the major holidays. Although with her big heart and over-flowing generosity, I imagined it was partly because she wanted to open up her home to my mother and me and whomever else she deemed worthy of an invitation.

At 4:07 p.m. on the Fourth of July, we arrived on Mama D.'s block, parked down the street behind a long string of cars, walked along the sidewalk

toward the house and went up the stairs. Marcus saw us through the living room curtain and opened the door, flashing a huge grin. He shook his head.

"You know … you all have the distinguished honor of being the first ones here. Come in and make yourselves at home. My grandmother's in the kitchen, finishing up the potato salad." He kissed my cheek.

The TV was blaring in the living room with some ESPN baseball pregame show. I instantly recognized several of the show's announcers, in particular the African-American commentators, from when I had lived with Ariel and her parents. Her father had put his heart and soul into watching the Cubs whenever they played. So when they'd won the World Series in the fall of 2016, you would have thought that he'd just landed the largest jackpot in Powerball history.

Mama and I sat down on the couch in the living room. Marcus returned shortly after, holding a tray full of celery sticks, a creamy dip, cheese squares, and small crackers. Mama and I helped ourselves to some cheese and tidbits.

The doorbell rang, causing Marcus to set down the veggie tray. When he opened the front door, I was shocked to see it was Ariel.

She smiled. "I know, I know, you didn't expect to see me here. Marcus invited me as a surprise," she said as she came inside. "Sorry my parents couldn't make it. They're visiting with my dad's side of the family in Wisconsin."

I stood up to give my best friend a big hug. "I see you were finally able to keep a secret," I said. We both laughed. Ariel stood radiantly in the doorway, wearing a tightfitting dress. Her face was dolled up, and her hair looked freshly permed. She looked amazing.

"Guess what?" Ariel said, excited.

"What?"

"I just got a full-time job offer. You're looking at the newest intern at one of the top accounting firms downtown."

My jaw almost hit the floor. "That's amaaaz-ing, Ariel. I'm so happy for you!" I gave my friend another huge hug. I knew how much this job opportunity had meant to her. Starting from the day I'd first met her, Ariel had always been good with numbers. It was her lifelong dream to become an accountant and eventually a CPA. The timing could not have been more perfect. With her and Tommy considering marriage, having a promising career would allow them both a chance at what some said was the fading American dream.

The doorbell chimed a second time. Marcus called out from the back of the house, asking if I would see who was at the door. When I opened it, standing on the porch flanked by a mysterious woman was none other than Pastor E.L. Tompkins himself. It was common knowledge among his congregation and even the surrounding community that the pastor was not married, so I wondered who this woman was that he was comfortable enough to bring her into Mama D.'s house.

She had flawless caramel skin and shoulder-length hair, and the black dress she wore left little to the imagination. It was tightfitting from the top of her shoulders, cut high around the thickness of her thighs. Her cleavage pushed up and out like it was starving for air. I was sure if Mama D. felt this woman was dressed inappropriately, she would have no problem in telling Pastor Tompkins so in private.

"Lula, good to see you again, my sister. This is my date, LaShonda."

"Nice to meet you," I replied. "Mama D. and Marcus are in the back. Come on in, the rest of us are here—me, Mama, and my friend Ariel."

Pastor Tompkins and his date walked inside as I

crossed to the other side of the room and grabbed two chairs. I lowered the volume on the television and then offered the tray of hors d'oeuvres as they both sat down.

"You can smell that food all the way here in the living room," Pastor Tompkins said as he flashed his trademark smile. "I often brag to the congregation what a really good cook Delores is. And I'm so thankful that she often donates her time and talents to the church's food drives."

Mama nodded her head. "That's a good thing you're doing for the community, Pastor. There are so many homeless people living in Chicago now, many without any food to eat." Mama laughed. "Don't ask me how I know."

"Thank you, Ella Mae. We certainly do whatever we can. The church has been a pillar of the community for over thirty years, starting with the original pastor, Wade E. Phillips, God rest his soul. And as the Good Book instructs us so wisely, to whom much is given, much is also required. So we're committed to doing our part to help people."

Marcus came walking out of the kitchen, carrying a stack of plates into another room. Directly behind him was Mama D., wiping her hands on her white apron. She looked as healthy and vibrant as I'd ever seen her. She was even moving about without the use of her cane. She grinned broadly as she shuffled into the living room.

"Good afternoon, everybody. I'm so glad you all could make it." Mama D. immediately drew her gaze to Pastor Tompkin's date.

"Delores, this here is my date, Ms. LaShonda Bishop."

LaShonda stood up to shake Mama D.'s hand. "It's a pleasure to meet you, Mama D. I've heard so much about you. E.L. is always bragging about what a wonderful congregation he has."

Mama D. nodded agreeably and smiled. "Well, he told you right, sweetheart. I've been a member as long as I've lived in this house. E.L. is not only my pastor, but we consider him a good friend as well. It's nice to meet your acquaintance. Now if you all will excuse me, I need to check on my grandson and see how he's coming along with setting the dining room table. He's slower than molasses and the food is almost ready."

Mama D. turned and ventured toward the back of the house. Pastor Tompkins's date reared back against her seat and hiked one leg over the other. "So, E.L. tells me that you ladies are community activists. How's that working out for you?"

How's that working out for you? It took only a few seconds for me to realize that this woman must have been out of touch with reality. Or maybe it was because … despite the fact that she was black herself, she did not identify with the plight of average black folks.

"We're off to a slow but promising start. There's a lot of work to be done, but I wouldn't have it any other way."

"Well, that's very admirable of you." LaShonda's gaze swept the room. "All of you. Good luck with what you're doing."

Marcus sauntered into the living room and made the announcement that the food was finally ready. He seemed to have been in a particularly good mood, because he was rapping like it was the start of some music video. He could be so silly at times. But I needed that. His offbeat humor worked to balance out the seriousness that the rest of my life had apparently been gripped by.

The five of us followed Marcus into the dining room, where everything looked quite magnificent. The setting. The dinnerware. The hand-carved chairs Mama D. had told me she'd purchased online. After joyously taking it all in, I straightened my skirt and took a seat between Mama and Ariel.

Pastor Tompkins and his date sat on the other side, leaving both ends of the mahogany table open for Marcus and his grandmother. Minutes later, Marcus brought the food in. First a large tray of barbeque ribs, chicken, turkey tips and hot links, followed by macaroni and cheese, spaghetti, potato salad, baked beans, corn on the cob, and pasta salad. Mama D. came in shortly after with a pitcher of iced tea and several two-liter bottles of soda.

"Pastor, we'll let you do the honor of saying a quick blessing before the food gets cold," Mama D announced.

"Be glad to, Delores." Pastor Tompkins allowed his eyes to do a quick sweep of the room. "Let us all bow our heads in prayer. Heavenly Father, we thank you for bringing us here safely into the home of Delores and Marcus today. We thank you for the food we are about to receive and ask that you bless it, and allow it to nourish our bodies. We ask that you bless the hands that have prepared it, Dear Lord. And that once this joyous occasion is over, we can all safely return to our places of residence. To you, and only to you, do we give praise. Amen."

Mama D. glanced around quickly. "Oh, I almost forgot. Afterward … I've got dessert for everyone, 7UP pound cake, peach cobbler, and ice cream."

"That sounds really good, Ms. Whitaker. I'll be sure to have some before I leave out of here," Ariel said.

Dishes of food were passed around family-style. There wasn't a whole lot of talking because everyone was so busy digging in. I couldn't blame them—Mama D. was such an excellent cook. I wondered if she'd possibly missed her calling as either a renowned chef or the owner of a successful restaurant somewhere. After dinner, she excused herself from the table and invited LaShonda to go and see her Annie Lee figurine collection.

When they were finished in the other room, and after Marcus came back from checking his phone for messages, everyone filed back into the dining room for dessert. Pastor Tompkins laid a napkin across his lap as he cut into a piece of peach cobbler.

"So, I heard through the grapevine that your music career is going quite well, Marcus. But just in case things don't work out long-term, do you have something to fall back on? You know … like a trade, a skill, or a college degree?"

"I did some college. But I'm like, hey … you

only live once. And I decided a while back that I'm going to pursue my dreams no matter what. Because when I die—I don't want to leave behind any regrets. In the meantime, I'm able to put food on the table, help Mama D. pay the bills, and take care of the house. I figure I can always go and get a job if necessary."

Pastor Tompkins was quiet for a moment before his eyes locked onto mine. "Lula, I understand you're a teacher by day when you're not out there fighting crime. Is that correct?"

I nodded. "Yes, that's correct. I feel really blessed to be able to work with two of my greatest passions, while getting paid for one of them."

"That *is* a blessing. And in your fight for justice, you would be wise to study what our great civil rights leaders did in their day. Although we have a long ways to go, we could not have made it this far had it not been for their courage and bravery."

"I feel forever indebted to them, along with American heroes like Harriet Tubman. But with all due respect, I feel like, today, our approach needs to be different."

Pastor Tompkins smiled as he wiped his mouth with his napkin. "I'll let you all in on a little secret. My father was also a minister, as was my grandfather. My father marched with Dr. King in 1965 during the three days from Selma to Montgomery. He along with the rest of the marchers were met with violent resistance. But ultimately, they achieved their goal of getting our people registered to vote in the South. I have some of the pictures of the march in my office at the church."

Marcus chimed in, "Well, we just see things a little different today, Pastor. No disrespect to anyone past or present, including yourself. But marching just ain't working today. Do you see all the unarmed people of color getting gunned down today? Nothing's being done about it. I'm so sick and tired of—"

Pastor Tompkins raised a hand. "Your generation is the most fearless generation we've had, Marcus. And it would be a great achievement if you could come together, combine your efforts and demand to be treated as equal Americans under the law. In no way am I saying that what you and Lula are doing is wrong. I'm just letting you know what worked for our people during the Civil Rights era. Back in my father's day."

Mama D. hobbled back into the room to join the conversation. Due to complications from her diabetes, she had skipped dessert and had been in the kitchen putting leftover food away. She looked tired. She looked like standing for most of the day had finally taken its toll on her. Slowly, she plopped down into a dining room chair holding an envelope.

"Marcus, how come you didn't tell me I had this letter come in the mail?"

Marcus stood up, came from the opposite end of the table and studied the envelope as Mama D. held it out in front of him. "It says it's from a law firm. You in some kind of trouble, Grandma?"

"If I am … it's because of you," Mama D. replied, laughing.

Marcus shrugged. "No, seriously, I left it on top of the mantel yesterday. I thought you had already seen it."

Mama D. blew out a big breath and began to tear open the envelope. For several minutes she seemed lost in reading its contents. Then she smiled and rested the palm of her hand across the top of her chest.

"Are you all right, Delores?" Pastor Tompkins asked, seeming concerned.

"Oh, my God. I don't believe this," Mama D. murmured.

"What is it, Grandma?" Marcus asked.

"This letter states that my aunt in Alabama,

who I hadn't spoken to in years, has passed. She'd taken possession of a large parcel of land said to be worth a lot of money. It was supposed to be mine after my mother died. Well, it says in this letter that in my aunt's will, the land was left to me as her only heir."

Pastor Tompkins jerked his chin forward. "Sounds like she decided to do the right thing before she passed on. So, congratulations, Delores. It just goes to show, of course: when you sow good seeds, good things happen for you."

Mama D. inserted the letter back into the envelope. "This is gonna call for a trip down there to Huntsville. Believe you me, I'll be calling these attorneys first thing after the holiday weekend is over. All I want is what's rightfully mine, nothing more, and without any hullabaloo!"

I watched as Mama D. swelled with joy and happiness. If anyone deserved to have some truly good fortune, no matter how late in life, it was her. Marcus had often told me about good deeds she had done that hardly anyone knew about. Like the time she'd bought food, clothing and Christmas presents for a woman across the street who had lost her job and was having a hard time receiving unemployment benefits. Or the time she'd allowed members of the church, a battered woman and her two children, to stay here in this house until they could get back on their feet.

Mama D. had rarely talked about her aunt in Alabama. Marcus himself had even confirmed this to me during one of our late-night evenings watching lightning bugs from the porch while talking. Although she showed no outward hostility or sadness about being estranged from one of her only living relatives, inside, somehow, you just knew it was tearing Mama D. apart.

Marcus stood up and rubbed the palms of his hands together. "I say we celebrate the good news my grandmother has gotten by having some fun tonight. By playing a round of Monopoly." Marcus put his hand to his ear. "Do I have any takers? Sounds like I heard some yeses floating somewhere around this room."

Ariel grinned. "Sure, Marcus. Why not? I love Monopoly. That's all me and my parents played when I was a kid."

"Pastor, Ms. Bishop?"

"Yes. Count us in, Marcus."

"Good. Then Monopoly it is! Besides, Grandma, if you're going to be the owner of some commercial land down in the great state of

Alabama, you might as well start practicing now." Marcus went to a closet in the hall and returned with the game. He lifted the cover, took out all the pieces and set them directly in front of Mama D.

No one left the house until almost ten o'clock. For at least the last two or three hours, no one had debated whether the best way to fight injustice was to march, protest, or take a much more progressive approach. We were just a gathering of different people coming together under one roof, enjoying each other's company.

As far as I was concerned, we were family.

CHAPTER 15

My mother and I, still in our nightgowns, sat in my apartment's living room just after sunrise. We laughed and told each other stories, as we would often do. Stories from her childhood on the plantation, and from mine. And then there were the games. Games we'd played as children to ease the pain of oppression and help to pass the time. My favorite game had always been about the Bogeyman, a game where one of the children in the slave quarters pretended to be an evil spirit and attempted to catch the others.

If I pretended not to cherish having a day off and spending these moments with Mama, I'd be lying. The more time we spent in this modern world, the more I could see us being apart. The pace of this century had been so much faster than what we were used to. Now that I was working, and Mama had found her a job, mostly, we would see each other only at night, or on weekends.

Even Marcus was out of town. He offered to accompany Mama D. during her trip to Huntsville, Alabama to see about her inheritance. I glanced at my watch and saw that it was a quarter of eight. I needed to get dressed. At nine a.m. I had a guest appearance on the *Vick and Tammy Morning Show* on FM radio. It was a new and progressive radio station here in the Midwest, which catered to a demographic of eighteen- to thirty-year-olds. Marcus knew one of the station's program directors and had put in a good word, which had led to the interview.

I walked toward the couch and pulled on the drawstring to open the curtains. To my surprise, the first thing I noticed was not the luminous rays of sunshine cascading through the window, but a small hole. A bullet hole with a spiderweb of cracks surrounding it.

"Mama, did you see this? This bullet hole?"

Mama got up from where she sat at the end of the sofa and walked closer to the window.

"It's my first time seeing that. It must have just happened, because it wasn't there yesterday."

Mama rubbed her hand over the opening. You could feel a small breeze blowing through the hole. "I watched kids play outside on the sidewalk yesterday. If it had been there, I would have seen it," Mama added.

I had seen my share of police dramas while living with Ariel and her parents. Immediately I looked down at the floor, scanning the carpet, then at the wall opposite the living room window, which was in the kitchen. I rushed across the room and observed a hole in the wall directly above the refrigerator. I figured the bullet must have lodged itself in the wall.

I turned toward Mama. She shook her head and appeared crestfallen. "We need to call the police, baby girl. It ain't safe for us here. We progressed to freedom. But we still in danger."

"Mama, before we jump to conclusions, let's talk to the police. For all we know it could have been a stray bullet meant for someone else. Not that that makes the situation any better. But we can't keep running. At some point, we've got to deal with these issues head-on."

Mama turned away and then sat on the couch. "When you lived with Ariel and her family, you didn't have this problem, Lula. Maybe we need to move to where they live."

"There was crime in Hyde Park. Maybe not to the extent there is around here. Besides, we can't afford to move there yet. With my salary as a substitute teacher and your minimum-wage job, this is the best we can do for now."

I went and sat down next to my mother. "Just give me some time, Mama. Somehow I'll get us out of here. But first, there's work that needs to be done."

My mother drew a deep breath and slowly nodded in agreement. "I just don't want nothing to happen to you, or me. I done already lost one child. You all I got now. Don't want to lose two. All you see on television, every night I watch the news, is shootings and death. We killing our own kind more than we ever did." Mama reared back against the couch's brown cushion.

"It's terrible, I know. And I don't have to tell you how I feel. That enough is not being done to combat inner-city violence. Of course, we didn't have TV on the Mansfield Plantation, but it would appear to me that even white folks are now killing each other more than they did back then, not counting the Civil War."

I leaned over and kissed Mama on her forehead. "I'll be back later. I've got that radio station interview I told you about. Maybe it'll be a start in the right direction," I said.

I left out of the apartment and got in my car. On my way to the station's main office in the South Loop, all I could think about was my mother's safety. Not once did I want to insinuate that the bullet hole in the window could have been a warning from someone who did not care for the work that I was doing. But I didn't care who I was pissing off. I was going to continue, undeterred.

I parked my car and walked into the building that served as the main office for the station. Immediately a receptionist greeted me on the first floor, wearing a headset of some kind. She smiled. "Good morning, how may I help you?"

"Good morning, my name is Lula Darling. I'm here as a guest on *The Vick and Tammy Morning Show*."

"You're punctual. That's a very good thing, because not many of our guests are. Please take the first elevator bank on your left to the second floor. As soon as you get off, you'll see the studio."

"Thank you."

As I made my way to the second floor, I felt my

stomach rumble in a wave of anxiety. First the bullet hole in the window, and now here I was about to speak to an audience of hundreds of thousands of people—further putting my name and agenda out there for all of Chicago to hear. I imagined that this interview and other public appearances like it could be putting me in clear and present danger.

To quell some of this fear, if not all of it, I thought of a biblical verse that had been ingrained in me ever since I was a child roaming the grounds of the Mansfield Plantation. Romans 8:28–31, which clearly states: "If God is for us, who can be against us?" I kept repeating to myself over and over again that God had brought Mama and me into the future for a reason, for a purpose.

The elevator door opened. Immediately across the hall was a large floor-to-ceiling glass window with a man and a woman wearing headsets and sitting behind a huge console. I assumed them to be Vick and Tammy, the popular morning hosts. I pushed open the heavy glass door of the studio. Vick was talking live on the air; he jerked his chin forward to acknowledge my presence. He was NFL stocky, with a mustache, beard, and dreads that hung over his shoulders and the colorful plaid shirt he wore. Tammy, to his right, was a very beautiful woman; her hair was coiffed, cut cute and short. Her butterscotch-colored skin looked flawless from where I stood.

Vick pressed a button and then removed his headphones. "You must be Lula Darling?"

I nodded and smiled. "Yes. I am."

"Come on around. We have a seat for you. Nice to meet you in person. I've heard quite a bit about you," he said.

His female cohost stood up and smiled. "Hi, Lula, pleased to meet you. Thanks for coming on our show this morning. Tammy Vazquez," she said in an unmistakable Spanish accent, extending her hand. I sat between them behind the huge console. In front of my face was a black microphone. Behind me was a large window overlooking Michigan Avenue.

"So, Marcus, who is a friend of mine, told me about the good work you're doing. And I asked him to talk to you about being on our show. How are you doing this morning?"

I nodded. "Good. Every day I wake up I consider it a blessing. No matter what happens during the day, I try to remain positive. So I'm good!" I looked at both Vick and Tammy. "And thank you guys for allowing me to be on your show."

Vick nodded. "No doubt. No doubt. We always have different guests, different artists, promoting their music and whatnot. So it was actually refreshing to have someone like yourself who wants to do good in the community and help stop all the senseless violence that's occurring in the city. And so, are you ready to be live on the air this morning?"

"I am. A little nervous, but I'm ready."

"Good. Because in about five minutes I'm going to introduce you. I'll be asking a series of questions. Just relax. The interview will be in a conversational format. Tammy and I will be taking turns with the questions, and all you have to do is simply reply with your answers. Don't worry, pretend it's only the three of us talking in the studio and there is no one else listening. I had to do exactly *that* my first few times on the air."

I took a deep breath. Vick glanced over at Tammy, and she nodded that she was ready to go back live after the commercial break. Vick helped me slip the headphones that lay in front of me over my head. Then he positioned the microphone low enough so that I could speak into it.

"Good morning again, Chicago. This is the portion of *The Vick and Tammy Morning Show* where we bring on a live guest to discuss relevant topics of the day. This morning's guest is a young lady whose name you might have heard before. She was the valedictorian of a citywide graduation at Soldier Field last year. The first of its kind in the city since…?" Vick briefly looked over at Tammy.

"Nineteen thirty-nine," she whispered.

"The first of its kind since … apparently, nineteen thirty-nine," Vick repeated. "But she didn't stop there. She's recently embarked on a new career as a special education assistant. And now, she's taken on the task of helping to fight Chicago's street violence. Welcome, Lula Darling, to *The Vick and Tammy Morning Show*."

"Thank you for having me."

"Lula, you have some really impressive credentials, already quite outstanding for someone your age. So tell us … how did you get started as an activist?"

"Well, I come from a humble background, where an emphasis on family was really important. We didn't have much in the way of financial or material wealth. But we had each other. We loved one another, and I realized early on that with all of us on the same page, so to speak, heading toward the same goal, collectively, there was nothing that we could not achieve. So it really hurts to see what's going on out here today. Young people killing each other, with no sense of self-worth or purpose. That is the reason why I'm determined to do all I can to hopefully put an end to it. Because at the end of the day, after the marches and protests are over, I just don't see a lot getting done."

Vick smiled and nodded. "I see. That's very admirable of you. There are a number of young people involved in the political process. We saw a lot of that in some of the recent presidential elections, how social media played a huge role in galvanizing people toward the candidate or political party of their choice. But I don't recall seeing any other young people around your age, barely in your twenties, as plugged in and ready to make a difference as you appear to be. What goals do you have to help achieve what it is you're planning to do?"

"A lot of this violence we're seeing is driven by gangs, and the drugs that are pouring into our communities. I personally feel that what we've done so far has obviously not been effective enough. And so, what I'd like to do is to create a new movement. One that has so many people working toward certain goals, one that has so many people putting never-before-seen pressure on our legislators and major corporations, which says that we will not yield in our demands until they do right by us. It is our right as Americans to live in generally safe communities and to have equal access to employment opportunities."

Tammy nodded her head. "It sounds like you have a very well-thought-out plan, Lula. You're young, so it should be easier for you to engage young people everywhere. I think today, some people often look at older career politicians, and these so-called leaders, as no longer being hungry to serve the will of the people, but merely self-serving."

"So, in a nutshell, what you're saying, Tammy, is that Lula here, by just starting out, has not been tainted," Vick chimed in and laughed.

"Yes, Vick. In so many words, that is exactly what I'm saying."

"Lula, I had a question for you," Tammy said.

"Sure."

"Are your efforts mainly focused on what's happening in the African-American community, or are they spread over various ethnic boundaries? I ask because there are a lot of people in the Latino community that listen to our show. Of course, Chicago is still very segregated compared to a lot of other cities around the country."

"Yes, ma'am. That's a good question. And the answer is an emphatic yes. Although I am based in the black community, I want and need help from everyone, whether they are black, brown, white or whatever. Some of the problems we see may be rooted in certain communities. But to a lesser extent, there are some problems that every community faces, increasingly so."

Vick shifted in his chair, then turned toward me and pulled his microphone closer to himself. "Lula, if you would, give us some examples of the problems that you're referring to. I want to make sure that our listeners have a clear understanding of exactly what it is you're talking about."

"Well, for instance, on the South and West Sides you have drive-by shootings, robberies, murders done by rival gang factions. For anyone who watches the news, these crimes have been festering on the South and West Sides of the city for far too long. Now, you're starting to hear about them on the North Side more often. There are certain drugs prevalent in the black community. And there are other drugs that are prevalent in the white community. So there needs to be a collective effort among all people, among all ethnicities, to solve this problem. There is strength in numbers. I believe that once a blueprint has been set for success, it will be easier for future generations to take a stand if necessary. But the time is now. Things are getting much worse."

Vick nodded. "They certainly appear to be. That was very well stated. And before we end this morning's show, there are two things we'd like to say to you. One, we'd like to have you back on the show in the future to let us know how things are working out with everything we've talked about. Two, we here at the station would like to do our part in helping you with your efforts."

Vick reached underneath the console and pulled a small envelope from a leather backpack. "So with that being said, I have here in my hand a check for five thousand dollars we'd like to donate to your cause. Something to help you get started with on your courageous and awe-inspiring journey."

My eyes went wide. I was astounded as Vick handed me the check. I pushed back from the console and stood, fighting back tears of joy as I hugged him and then Tammy. Lord knows I had all the desire in my heart to fight for change, but the one thing I did not have was enough money to start making a difference. "Thank you!" I said to them both. "This money will be put to very good use. Thank you very much!"

A moment later Vick went into another commercial break. "Be sure to tell Marcus we want first dibs on that new CD of his as soon as it drops," he said.

"I'll make sure he brings the very *first* copy of his record directly to you guys, gift-wrapped," I replied. I put the check inside my purse and sauntered through the glass door of the studio.

The fact that this radio station had enough consciousness to produce a morning show to address the needs of a hurting community was extremely admirable. I'd come here specifically to get the word out about what I was doing. But to leave this place holding a check to fund the Movement allowed me to see that I was not isolated in my beliefs. I was not alone in my search for justice and equality.

Someone else had believed in me too.

CHAPTER 16

I WAVED at the receptionist in the lobby, then walked out of the building onto South Michigan Avenue bristling with newfound enthusiasm. I could not wait to tell Marcus, Mama, and everyone else that I'd had the good fortune of being on the receiving end of such a large charitable donation. Sometimes you just had to wonder whether people around you openly supported you in what you were doing because it was the right thing to do, or because they truly believed that you could accomplish whatever it was that you were seeking. If it was the former, hopefully, after today, they would feel differently.

After leaving the South Loop area, I stopped by a small grocery store on the South Side. I had promised Mama that I would cook dinner at home for a needed change. Due to my being tired and stressed after work lately, we'd been eating mostly soups, salads, and anything else that could be heated and ready to eat within minutes. Besides, Mama was still working on her cooking chops and learning what she could by reading cookbooks and experimenting in the kitchen.

Once inside the store, I ventured down several aisles, picking up some ground turkey, potatoes, onions, a green pepper. At the end of one aisle, talking to one of the store clerks, I saw Mr. and Mrs. Thomas, the elderly couple that lived downstairs from Mama and me on the first floor. When the clerk walked away, Mr. Thomas turned, and I ducked into an adjacent aisle, not wanting to be noticed. I figured that I would simply wait and talk to my neighbors on some other occasion. For now, I just wanted to get home.

With my handbasket half-full, I headed toward the express lane. "Find everything you were looking for today?" A heavyset woman—reddish-pink shock of hair, silver stud in the center of her pierced tongue—said to me from behind the register and smiled.

"Yes. Just enough for today's dinner," I replied.

"Well, be sure to come back and see us, okay?"

She stared at me for several moments. Her eyes locked onto mine. She held my hand as if to make sure my change did not spill over when she gave it to me. If you had asked me six months ago what I had thought of this, I would have simply told you that she was just being friendly to a customer. But I was no longer naïve to believe that there wasn't an ulterior motive behind her kindness.

"I will, thank you."

I put the change in my wallet, one that I always carried with me in my purse, and then headed out into the parking lot. I opened the rear door of my car to set the bag of groceries on the backseat. There was the hum of an accelerating engine on my right. I looked up to see a black SUV with its window lowered, the barrel of a long gun pointed directly at me.

I flung myself onto the ground, slid beneath a gray car that had been parked next to mine. The sound of automatic gunfire was unmistakable as a volley of bullets penetrated my Nissan. My heart went racing. I was delirious and in a panic. I saw the feet of someone who had run out of the store and then heard what sounded like return fire. The SUV then sped off, its tires screeching, and veered out of the parking lot. I heard people running to my aid. I saw the black shoes of someone standing by the vehicle under which I had hidden. Then, whoever this person was, they crouched down onto the pavement, on their knees.

"Hey, are you all right? Were you hit?" A hand was extended to assist me. It was a man, his voice deep and sharp.

"I'm okay. I think."

"Let me help you get out from under there." I grabbed his hand, and he pulled me, my clothes scraping the asphalt surface. I got to my feet, wiped dirt and pebbles off my dress and looked around. "I work security for the store. I heard the shots and ran outside and returned fire. My name is Walter," he said over puffs of breath as he holstered a large black pistol.

I briefly glanced at my car and saw that the back window had been completely obliterated. There were also bullet holes in the trunk. My face flooded with heat. Surrounding me now was a small group of people, bystanders and perhaps witnesses. Among them were Mr. and Mrs. Thomas, who had come out of the store.

"Lula? My God, child. Were they shooting at you?"

I nodded. "Yeah, I'm afraid so." I took a deep

breath as the sound of police sirens drowned out something else Mr. Thomas had said. I imagined what he and his wife, Doris, must have been thinking. I imagined them wondering if I had lost my mind and whether I would ultimately pay the price because of it.

The security guard clapped a hand on my shoulder. "I need you to come inside for your safety. Plus get you cleaned up. The police can talk to you in the store," he announced. I followed the guard inside and watched as he retrieved a chair and set it in front of a row of vending machines. I was so upset that it felt like every ounce of my blood had rushed to my brain.

Before I sat down, I peered out the window into the parking lot. There were several cops placing evidence markers where shell casings lay. Several more policemen, including two plainclothes cops, came walking into the store.

"You okay?" one of them asked.

"Yeah, I'm okay. Just a little shaken."

"You recognize the shooters or get a good look at them?"

"All I know was that it was a black SUV. The guy pointing the gun out the window was black as well. But everything happened so fast … I did not get a good look at him."

The officer stood before me and jotted down details as I spoke. Within earshot, I overheard another cop asking the store manager if there were any surveillance cameras around the store. The policeman who had interviewed me asked for my name and address. "Any idea why they would want to harm you?"

"It could be because I'm an activist. I've been opposed to all of the violence and drugs that are ravaging our community. I imagine they now want to silence me."

The cop nodded. "Believe me, you would not be the first. You got a way home?"

Before I could answer, Mr. Thomas, who had been standing with his wife nearby, quickly interceded. "Officer, my wife and I live downstairs from this young lady on Michigan Avenue. We would be glad to take her home."

"All right, that's fine. But I'll follow you once we're finished to make sure the three of you get home safe."

The policeman started talking to several other people who claimed to have witnessed the shooting. Suddenly, from the back of the store, I saw a young man being led away in handcuffs. Curious, I tapped Walter on the shoulder to find out if there was something else going on here, something else I'd missed. "Who's that?" I asked.

Walter watched the police as they escorted the guy toward the front of the store, then he gazed back at me. "Just a thug who thought he could take advantage of the situation and steal something. I guess he thought no one was paying attention. Loss prevention had their eyes on him even before the shooting started."

A short while later, the police appeared to have concluded their questioning. I pulled out my cell phone and sent a group text to everyone that I held dear to me. I wanted to be the first to let them know what had happened. More importantly, I wanted to let them know that I had not been harmed.

Moments later Walter left my side and went to confront the alleged shoplifter as he stood near the front of the store. While holding the suspect's arm, the police asked the manager on duty several additional questions. The amateur sleuth in me began to wonder if there had been some connection between this guy and the murderous goons in the parking lot.

Walter stood in front of the shoplifter, grinning

menacingly. Immediately the young man took in Walter's imposing size. The security guard appeared to be at least six-three or six-four and had a monstrous build. He took no shame in taunting the man in custody. "I seen you come in here on other occasions. I guess you called yourself casing the store. Well, looks like it done caught up to you now ain't it?"

The young man shook his head, clearly annoyed. "Nah, man, I'm good. You don't know nothing 'bout me, homeboy. I gets down for mine … I can get wit you. I don't care how big you are."

"You threatening me?" Walter snapped. He furrowed his brow. "I'll get with you, too."

"Man, ain't nobody scared of you. All you is—is a wannabe—a sucka punk rent-a-cop!"

The officer holding him jerked him violently. "That's enough. You shut your mouth!"

For some odd reason the young man, struggling to stay upright, suddenly trained his gaze on me. He was wearing a gray hoodie and sagging jeans, his eyes feral like a wild animal. "Introduce me to that shorty over there before you haul me off to jail," he said sharply.

Another cop walked over. "No one wants to hear you run your mouth, Romel. Not me. Not the young lady you're laying your eyes on right now. But even so, if you *do* get some action tonight, it ain't gonna be with a woman, I can tell you that." The officer jerked his chin. "We're good now." Then he pointed. "Get him out of here."

For a few minutes, I stood frozen near the store's security sensors, fighting an army of emotions. There was a part of me that hated seeing another young person of color being whisked away, where the nation's prison-industrial complex waited.

I felt broken for those who were wrongly convicted, because the wheels of justice turned ever so slowly—if at all—for people who happened to look like I did. So I watched as they escorted the man outside and placed him headfirst in the back of a police car. One of the cops slammed the door and then looked back and grinned. "We'll be in touch, Walter."

Standing now at the store's entrance, Walter looked satisfied and returned the smile. "All right. We good, then."

CHAPTER 17

THEY SAY that during times of stress and adversity is when a person's character is made stronger. So the thought of walking out of this convenience store, to me, felt like a captive being ordered to walk the plank on the high seas. With my heart racing, my palms beading perspiration, I followed the remaining police officers outside. Flanking me were the Thomases. I imagined that under the circumstances, the elderly couple had to have been nervous, too.

I got in the backseat of their car, an older-model Buick with a sticker on its rear bumper, which read: I VOTE FOR DEMOCRATS. Mama had once told me, after having a conversation with Mrs. Thomas, that her husband blamed politicians on both sides for the state that the country was in. The fact that there was more than one political party gave rise to instant conflict, she'd told Mama. Nevertheless, they never missed an opportunity to cast their ballot.

As we slowly pulled out of the parking lot, I turned back and took one last look at my car. I wondered if the damage was even worth getting repaired, or if I would have to go in search of another vehicle. For several minutes, the mood inside of the Thomases' car was pensive. I imagined that they were wondering what to say to break the silence without coming across as judgmental. It was almost as if I were a kid being picked up by grandparents after being sent home from school for disciplinary reasons.

"Why don't you and your mother consider moving?" Mr. Thomas asked as he looked in the rearview mirror. I glanced down. My cell phone had repeatedly been buzzing. We were already around the corner from the building, so I allowed the calls to go to voicemail.

I peered out both sides of the car, wary of seeing that ominous black SUV again. "We haven't even been here for that long," I told him. "But I imagine we'll be able to move in due time." I looked out the back window and saw a police car within a short distance.

Mr. Thomas reached forward and turned down the volume of the Buick's radio. "In my opinion, crime has gotten way out of hand. Add to that all the taxes and other high costs of living, it's no wonder why people are fed up and leaving. Doris and I are talking about moving into a retirement community. Someplace where the weather is beautiful, and you don't have to worry about getting shot just walking out your door."

"I hope that we can do the same one day, Mama and I. But for now, we have to do the best we can. Crime, of course, is only one part of a much larger problem, Mr. and Mrs. Thomas. That's why I am so committed. That is why I want to be a part of the solution."

Mr. Thomas shook his head. In the rearview mirror, his eyes appeared again, sharp and focused. "Even if it kills you, huh? As you can see, plain as day, it is *dangerous* … what you're doing, Lula, taking on that kind of responsibility."

I remembered having lived through danger and adversity when I was a child, beyond what most people today could ever imagine. I could tell this lovely couple the truth about who I really was. I could tell them that I was born before even they had entered the world. But I decided to digress instead.

I nodded. "I know what you're saying, and I appreciate it. But running away from the problem is only allowing it to get worse. Yes, they actually attempted to *take my life* today. And that is what they want, to either kill me or put enough fear in me that I give up the cause. But I'm not going to do that. I'm not going to give them the satisfaction of making me throw in the towel."

Moments later we pulled in front of the building. I got out of the backseat and then opened the door for Mrs. Thomas. I could tell that sitting in the car, even for this relatively short ride, had made her body stiffen to the point where she needed some assistance. In the back of my mind, I hoped that what had happened today motivated the Thomases to speed up their plans for relocation. They deserved better. They deserved to live their golden years not in a warzone, but in a place that did not make national headlines for all the wrong reasons.

"Thank you for the ride home," I told them as we walked into the building.

They both stopped when they got in front of their door. Mr. Thomas turned to me and said,

"You take care of yourself, Lula. You or your mother need anything, just let us know."

I nodded. "I will."

As Mr. Thomas inserted his key in the door, I glanced at my cell phone. There was a text from Marcus saying that he was concerned, could hardly concentrate while driving, and that he and Mama D. were already on I-65N, heading back up from Huntsville. It was not simply because of the failed attempt on my life today, but apparently because Mama D. had finished signing whatever papers she'd needed to sign in order to receive her inheritance.

I looked inside my purse to make sure I still had the check from the radio station, then headed up the stairs. Before I even got close to the apartment, I could hear music in the hallway. I inserted my key, opened the door, and saw Mama straight away in the living room. She was sitting on the couch, her eyes closed, her head swaying as if calming herself into a place of inner peace. She was humming a song that I did not recognize.

"You might have called," she said softly, her eyes shiny as she stared at me while turning down the volume on a boombox. It was a token of appreciation that Marlene Baker had given her after the incident at the restaurant.

"I'm sorry. I was talking to the police. There was so much going on. And then the Thomases brought me home." I walked toward my mother to let her know how sorry I was for not calling, even though I'd sent her a text. In this very moment, I wondered if I'd also fallen victim to this new digital world, where most personal communication was now done electronically, if at all.

Mama exhaled deeply. "Well, at least you were not harmed. I've come to realize that this is what you want to do with your life and that I can't talk you out of it. I don't know why I expected otherwise. You're my child. Knew you from the day you were born, of course. You are just like your father. He had that same fighting instinct that eventually cost him his life on that plantation."

Mama shifted on the couch, which we had moved away from the window, then stared back at me. "So I say all that to say … I'm not going to worry no more, Lula, hard as that may be. I'm going to leave it strictly in God's hands. I'm going to pray that His guidance and hedge of protection never leaves you—or me, for that matter."

I smiled and took a seat next to my mother on

the sofa. I reached for her hand, clasping it within the center of mine, and rested my head on her shoulder. "I thought you'd be angry. I thought you'd even be ready to leave Chicago for a more tranquil setting," I said.

Mama clasped my hand between both of hers. "I've said my piece, my child. Ain't much more there is to say.

After that, I remained still. I closed my eyes and simply meditated on my mother ultimately giving me her blessing. I was thankful that she was not going to stand in the way of what I believed to be my true life's purpose.

Suddenly a gentle knock interrupted the silence. I rose from the couch and walked toward the door. Looking through the peephole, I could see that it was Ariel. When I opened the door, she entered my apartment and pulled me into her embrace. "I'm so glad to know you weren't shot. I was able to leave work early using some emergency family leave. This is so crazy!" she said, shaking her head.

I shrugged. "I can't complain, Ariel. This is what I signed up for. This is the occupational hazard that comes with being an activist."

Ariel tossed back her hair and smiled as she thumbed away a tear. I knew my friend almost better than anyone and could see her going into a meltdown. "You were always the stronger one between us, Lula."

Stronger.

I had to think about that for a moment. I had to let the word marinate in the part of my brain that was responsible for the emotions that seemed to wash over me like a tide washes up on shore. And it was no surprise to me why Ariel would feel this way. After all, our lives as children could not have been any more different.

I gave my best friend another hug and patted the small of her back. "No crying. You're supposed to hold it together. Do you remember the motto we made in high school? The phrase that lifted our spirits whenever we felt all alone in the world? 'We are strong. We are one. There is nothing we fear under the sun'?"

Ariel wiped her eyes, smearing her mascara. "Yeah, I remember. I'm just worried I'll lose you. Honestly speaking, you are the sister I never had, Lula—up until the day we first met."

"Now you've got me teary-eyed, Ariel. Girl, come all the way in," I said. "Mama's in the living room." Ariel walked away from the doorway and greeted Mama as she stood up from the couch. "Hi, Ella Mae."

The three of us sat down while Ariel removed her compact mirror from her purse and dabbed her cheeks with tissue. "My parents have been trying to reach you all afternoon. They're on their way now, as we speak."

"I don't want to make them feel——"

Ariel shook her head. "Don't worry about it. You both are like our extended family. And family is supposed to come through for one another in times of need. In times exactly like this."

Ariel clasped her hands in front of her as she looked at Mama, then at me. "You know, I guess you could say that there's a silver lining in this horrible tragedy after all." She began to grin with that unmistakable smile of hers.

"How do you mean?" I asked.

"Well, after what happened to you earlier, my dad talked to a friend of his who knows a man who owns a nice brownstone not far from us in Hyde Park. The owner, as a favor to the guy both he and my dad knows, would like to offer you both a two-bedroom apartment for whatever amount you're paying here for rent."

Almost immediately after hearing those words, I

brightened in a cloud of disbelief. I didn't know what to say or how to respond. Ariel and her parents had already done so much for Mama and me. We'd need two more lifetimes just to pay back the kindness.

Ariel continued. "If you're going to be the next great twenty-first-century leader, fighting injustice, corruption, gangbangers, or whatever, you might as well do it from a nicer and safer neighborhood. Don't get me wrong, I know there're some good pockets here and there in this area, but ladies, this ain't one of 'em. Besides, it sounds like those thugs know where you live now."

Mama shifted in her seat. "Well, that's mighty kind of you and your family, Ariel. I'm not sure how Lula and I could ever repay you all for everything you've done. Maybe if I were to get another—"

"Don't worry about it. My dad always says that people need to get back to being compassionate, the way they used to be, instead of thinking about only themselves." Ariel shifted her gaze back and forth between Mama and me. "I've seen the apartment, and it's really nice. My dad emailed me several pictures of it that were sent to him this afternoon."

Mama nodded, then stood up and calmly walked into the bedroom. Ariel and I briefly looked at one another as she tried to pull up the pictures of the apartment on her cell phone. Then, a few seconds later, Mama returned to the living room comfortably fitted in her walking shoes, wearing her summer straw hat and her hair pulled into a knot at the base of her neck.

"When do we move?" she asked. "I'm not gonna miss the roaches in this building, nor will I miss everything else that goes on around here." Mama walked past Ariel and me, drew back the curtains on the window and pointed. "See this bullet hole right here? That is a constant reminder that it's time for us to go!"

Mama laughed, and so did Ariel and I. Maybe it was from watching the weekly sitcoms or conversing with people while at her job at Marlene Baker's restaurant—either way, Mama seemed to have developed her own coy sense of humor.

At times like this, I wanted to put aside everything that I knew I would face in the coming weeks, from this moment on. Ongoing scrutiny from the CIA, NSA, Department of Homeland Security, a clear and present danger from Chicago's most notorious gangs, and opposition from anyone who saw the Movement as a threat.

But my faith in God was bigger than any of

these perceived threats, or danger. And no matter what happened in the immediate future, I had already been blessed beyond measure to have the love of those around me. For that, I was eternally grateful.

ABOUT THE AUTHOR

ALEX DEAN is the author of *Restraining Order*, and *The Secret Life of Lula Darling.* He is an entrepreneur, former musician, and somewhat of a health enthusiast who enjoys being creative. He writes thrillers as well as other sub-genres of fiction and lives in Illinois with his family. For previews of his upcoming books and more information about Alex Dean, please visit alexdeanauthor.com.

Word-of-mouth is crucial for any author to succeed. **If you enjoyed this book, please consider leaving a review, even if it's only a line or two; it would make all the difference and would be greatly appreciated**.

ACKNOWLEDGMENTS

I would like to thank God for His many blessings, a heartfelt thanks to my wife and my parents for their valuable feedback, my children and family for their love and support. A big thanks to my in-laws for supporting my endeavors, and a tremendous thanks to my readers for your continued support.